Charge it to the Game 3:

Three Sides to Every Story

Keaidy Selmon

OTHER BOOKS BY KEAIDY SELMON

Charge it to the Game

Charge it to the Game 2: Tammy's Story

Charge it to the Game 4: Pride Comes B4
Destruction

The Chronicles of a Love Addict: A Love
Junkie's Journey from Suicidal to Saved

Somewhere Between Love & Misunderstanding

Shut Up & Finish Your Book Already

I am Capable of Success (available late 2022)

When a Woman's Fed Up (available late 2021)

She Fell in Love with a Boss

DEDICATION

For my grandmother: the gems that you deposited in me will not go to waste. I thank you for being a living, breathing, walking example of God's goodness and faithfulness. Thank you for all of your teachings.
Rest in peace mi amor.

For my forever best friend Damian Mazloomi.
Thank you for loving me and seeing things that I struggled to see in myself. Thank you for being a sanctuary – a safe place - while I grew into a better version of me. The way you loved me at my lowest inspired me to be who I am today. I will forever be grateful to everything you've been.
Rest easy baby.

Copyright © 2020 Keaidy Selmon

LexxiKhan Presents Publishing
www.LexxiKhanPresents.com

Ordering Information:
Quantity sales. Special discounts are available on quantity purchases by corporations, associations, and others. For details, contact the publisher at the web address above.

This book contains an excerpt from the next installment in the Charge It to the Game series. It may be edited or deleted prior to actual publication.

ISBN-13: 978-0-9600635-5-0

MESSAGE FROM THE AUTHOR

From the bottom of my heart, thank you so much for your love and support. Writing an urban fiction novel was something I only dreamed of doing for almost a decade, and the fact that I'm now not only doing it, but I'm encouraging others to follow their dreams also is an amazing feeling. Because of your support, you are helping to make the lives of our future generation of leaders easier. To find out more information and how you can help the cause to win back our youth, visit my website: Keaidy.com or Webuildexcellence.org **Disclaimer: This book does not glorify the street life. Although we call it a game, I want it to be clear that no one ever wins. Before you make the decision to 'play,' make sure you consider a very important question. How much would you risk if what you lost you had to Charge it to the Game?**

CHAPTER ONE

"Ugh," K.Y. grunted. "Let's just hurry up and get this shit over with."

K.Y. knew Isabella was not going to give up the information he desperately wanted without some sort of cost. Still, he wasn't expecting her to be so adamant about sleeping with him.

He was already having a hard time wrapping his mind around losing the love of his life and finding out that the love he gave her so freely and endlessly was all in vain.

"Don't cheat me," she said as she tugged on his shirt and led him to the elevator.

Just as the elevator doors opened, he felt the vibration of his iPhone in his pocket.

"Meet me in the room," he said as he looked at the screen and contemplated answering the blocked number that was calling him.

"Don't bullshit me," Isabella warned. "And don't take all night," she managed to say before the doors closed.

K.Y. didn't immediately answer the phone because only two people ever called his phone blocked, and one of them was with him when the call came through.

"Don't do it," Tamia Santiago's voice said sternly through the phone.

"Ha," K.Y. responded as he took a seat in the hotel lobby. "You really have a lot of nerve. I haven't talked to your ass in months, and you really think you can call me barking out orders. I always knew you were crazy, but this confirms it. You're crazy as hell," he said with a laugh.

"You don't understand," Tammy replied. "This is way deeper than you could ever imagine."

"That's so funny coming from you because from what I'm seeing, you've always kept shit at the surface level with me. Now, you want to tell me how deep shit is," he huffed.

Then, it hit him. Why, after all of this time, was Tammy suddenly calling him now?

"How the hell," he asked while he looked around.

"Even if I don't say anything, I know everything that goes on in these streets. If you go through with this, you'll be making a big mistake," Tammy responded

"The only mistake I ever made was loving and trusting you with yo' snake ass."

"Ouch. That was a little harsh, but I guess I deserve that. You're angry, and it's justified, so I'm not going to take it personally.

The woman in that room is not who you think she is. You don't know a thing about who you're dealing with. You want to be pissed off, then fine, but please do not go through with this."

"What's funny is that after all of these years, I don't know shit about you," K.Y fired back at her. "So I think you should be the last one pointing fingers at anyone."

"You're getting quick with these comebacks. It's kind of cute, but I need you to remember what I taught you and that -," Tammy said before an angry K.Y. cut her off.

"I'm done playing these fucking games with you. Save your phony ass compliments and details of shit you supposedly taught me. I'm a grown-ass man, and I can take care of my damn self. Now that your skeletons are coming out, you want to call and talk about things you taught me? That's not going to happen this time. Those days are gone, and so is that foolish ass nigga I used to be about you. I'm not falling for your shit again.

Nice try, but this time around you never planned that my feelings wouldn't be the same. Fuck you," K.Y spat before he disconnected the call.

***

"Good boy," Isabella said once K.Y. was in the room. "You actually do know how to follow directions sometimes."

"Shut up. I'm really not in the mood for this shit. Let's just take care of this and go our separate ways."

"Mira pendejo," Isabella snapped. "I don't know what your problem is, but this is my time, my game, and we are finally going to do everything my way. What the hell happened that suddenly has you so pissed off now anyway?"

"Your friend called," he said as he took off his sneakers.

"Fuck that bitch," she screamed. "She's bold as fuck. Shorty played both of us, so what the fuck could she possibly have to say to you after all of this time?"

"Just a bunch of bullshit like always," K.Y responded, hoping she would just drop the conversation.

"Well, just forget about her," she said as she sat down on the bed and began rubbing his back. "Tammy didn't realize what she had when she had you, so she shouldn't be able to have that much of an effect on you."

K.Y. knew her statement was true, but even after all of this time, he couldn't deny everything he still felt for her. For months he had been silently praying for a phone call or a visit from Tammy. Even though he said what he said, he wished things would have been different between them. He really missed the future he had imagined having with her.

"Now," Isabella said as she stood up from the bed and walked over to the T.V. to turn it off. "I'm going to tell you everything you've been dying to know about Tammy. I'll break everything down from the moment her father died, so you can see the bigger picture of everything. We can go over that later, but first, let me help you take that edge off," she said seductively. "I want to help you get out of your head for a minute."

K.Y. had been in such a bad mood that he never really took a look at just how good Isabella looked in the lingerie and red bottoms that she had been wearing. The red from the lace panties and bustier that she was wearing looked great on her mocha complexion.

"How exactly are you going to do that," K.Y. said as he laid back on the bed and tried to relax.

"I would say that we both would agree that I love to be in control," she said with a giggle. "Since we always do things by your rules, I want to change that up a little. I need you to be a good boy tonight," she said as she turned on some music on her phone and began dancing.

"You're not going to talk for the rest of the evening. Are we clear," she asked him.

He nodded.

"Good," Isabella responded before she walked over to her large overnight bag. "Oh, and you're going to do exactly what I tell you to do," she said as she laid two sets of handcuffs and a roll of pink duct tape on the bed.

CHAPTER TWO

Once Tammy was securely inside the limo that Jason had waiting for her, she allowed all of the tears that had been weighing her down to finally be released.

"I'm here whenever you're ready to open up and talk," Ms. Cruz said as she gently laid one hand on Tammy's knee.

Ms. Cruz hated funerals and, for that reason, decided not to attend. But she promised to be waiting for Tammy as soon as she got out.

"Will these feelings ever go away," Tammy managed to ask in between sobs. "Will I feel this guilt forever? Right now, I hate myself for being so selfish in those moments when my dad just wanted to spend with me. He took time out of his life to be with me that day, and all I could think about was getting out of there. I keep telling myself that if I had opened up more, maybe he would still be here. It wasn't hard for me to tell him that I loved him back or to talk about my feelings more. Either way, I wasn't in the mood, and I just shrugged him off. I hate myself for doing that. Now, I'll never get the chance. On the other hand, I tell myself that if I never talked him into one on one time, he wouldn't have even been in that spot. No matter how I think about that night, it just feels like it's all my fault. Will I ever get over the pain of losing my dad?"

"That's a choice that you have to be willing to make on your own. Happiness is not a place or destination; it is a choice. Once you've made that choice to get there, you have to continuously make the choice to remain happy. For now, all you have to do is cry. Cry until you don't have any tears left, and we can worry about happiness another day."

Tammy didn't protest. She slid closer to Ms. Cruz, laid her head in her lap, and she did just that.

***

The thought of going home after her father's funeral was just too much to bear for Tammy. Instead, she had the limo driver take her to a nice hotel and asked Jason to bring her things.

"I know this is tough," Jason said as he walked through the door with the mile-long list of things she had requested. "But we need to get back to business, and we need to do it now."

"What the hell Jason? I just lost my father, and the rest of my life is still kind of a mess. Do you really have to do this shit now? Can't I just enjoy a little time to myself peacefully?"

"No," he answered frankly. "Your dad has an entire dynasty that needs someone to restore some order to it, and that person is you. Let's go."

"Ok...well... doesn't my father have like a lieutenant or whatever position is next in this thing? Why the hell would I be taking over my father's shit? I've never done anything in this industry before. Why would niggas trust me to take over this shit now?"

The pressure was suddenly starting to overwhelm Tammy, and her usual calm demeanor was beginning to unravel.

"I can't do what my father did. I honestly don't' even know what all he did. How can I do my shit and his too?

Yo," Tammy said as she began struggling to catch her breath. "Why does it feel like I'm about to die right now? My heart is racing, and I can't breathe." She grabbed her chest as she gasped for air.

"Relax, Tee," Jason demanded as he ushered her over to the bed. "You're having anxiety attack right now. Lay back and close your eyes. Don't focus on anything else but your breathing right now."

Without protest, Tammy did precisely as she was told.

He put one hand on her chest and began telling her when to inhale and when to exhale. Once he saw that she was calming down, he started speaking again.

"Fear is a bitch, and you have every right to be scared right now. You're walking into something you feel you know nothing about, but believe it or not, your father has been grooming you for this since you came back into his life.

Yes, some street hustlers have a lineup like that, but your dad was way bigger than that. Your dad was in bed with old-school mafia niggas. They won't let just anyone sit at their table. It has to be someone from the family.

Your make-up vendor, that's also your dad's coke connect. The company you've hired for shipping and distribution is where your dad got his weed and all of his other drugs from. The company that handled your packaging is tied in with the politicians and dirty cops your dad had on payroll. Even though you didn't know it, you were sitting at the table earning their trust and loyalty for when this day came.

Your dad's job was just to oversee and make sure shit was running smoothly. You won't even have to touch the drugs if you don't want to. My job is to make sure other niggas do their job. All of your dad's legal businesses already have people over them. You just keep everyone in line and call all of the shots. That's it.

I'll be here for everything. I got you, and you got this."

She took a few more deep breaths before she opened her eyes and sat up.

"What if I don't want to do this? What if I just want to take time to mourn his death like a regular fucking human being? You know I talk a lot of shit, but I'm not built to run my father's organization. I just want a chance to feel normal for once."

"If you want all of the work that your father spent his whole life to build to go in vain, then you take all of the time that you need. If you want to have money to continue to live like you have been or so that the streets don't go crazy trying to take your father's throne, you need to get the fuck up, get dressed, and get over it and let's move.

I know it sounds rough, but that's just how shit is in this game. You have to have heart, but you certainly can't think with it or show it. All of Delino's men need to know what's going to happen next. Do you have any idea how many employees your father had that now don't know where their next meal will come from? In a minute, niggas are going to start going crazy, trying to take whatever they can to survive. It's bad enough that it's been three days. I wanted to give you some time, but you need to pull yourself together. This is not the Tammy I know, and I know for a fact that your father would not have wanted to see you acting like this either."

Tammy hated to admit it because more than anything, she just wanted to wallow in this moment, but knew he was right.

"I promised your father that I was going to see this all the way through, and I meant that.

In that bag," he said as he pointed to a pink bag that appeared to contain a dress, "is your outfit for tonight. It's a female suit and some shades to cover those puffy eyes of yours.

Tonight, do not play up your sex appeal. These niggas need to see a strong player that's going to keep shit going as smoothly as it has been.

Pull it together, Tammy; if they don't feel you now, then they never will. Don't blow it. I'm going to be downstairs. You have 20 minutes to meet me in the lobby, or I'm going to assume that sitting up here, playing the victim and crying like a little bitch means more to you than your father's legacy."

Without waiting for her response, he walked out and closed the door behind him.

***

"My father used to teach me all types of Chinese proverbs. It was a weird obsession of his. My favorite one is, 'when the winds of change blow, some people build walls and others build windmills," Tammy roared as she stood in front of the room of most of her father's key players.

"What the fuck does that have to do with my job or my fucking money," one man said with pure disgust as he stood up. "I've been in this game," he managed to say before Tammy abruptly interrupted him.

"Shut up and get the fuck out," Tammy demanded sternly.

Jason shot Tammy a piercing look. He knew that the men were going to have a hard time adjusting to the new change, but he didn't think it was going to start this rough.

"You can't make me leave. Do you have any idea who the hell I am to this organization," the man asked her as he stood up.

"Clearly," Tammy said as she walked over to where the man was standing, "it hasn't clicked to you exactly who the hell I am to this organization now. I have the power to promote, demote, and get rid of whoever the hell I want to." The two were standing face to face now. "As I was trying to say before I was rudely interrupted, I'm keeping everything the same as my father had it. That's how it will be, for now, unless I see any immediate reasons for change. If you want to keep your blocks and access to my product, I suggest you sit down and shut up. If that's not what you want, the door is that way," Tammy declared, pointing to the door of the warehouse they were in. "The choice is yours., motherfucker."

Without another word, the man sat back in his seat.

"I've heard great things about each and every one of you," Tammy lied as she made her way back to the front. "For that reason, I don't want to lose any of you. But because I was raised by a man who understood that no one could achieve greatness without first experiencing and accepting change, I have no problem moving this organization without anyone who does not want to be here. If any of you have a problem with me leading you and making sure we all eat as good if not better than we all have been, then please take this time to excuse yourself now."

Tammy waited a minute, but no one got up. "I'm going to assume that since all of your asses are still in my chairs, we're all on the same page now."

Without any other objections, Tammy continued on with her speech.

CHAPTER THREE

"Just call him," Ms. Cruz suggested. "You know you want to anyway."

"It doesn't matter," Tammy responded, not bothering to break her trance from her laptop. "I don't care to hear anything he has to say to me anymore."

"That's bullshit. You just can't handle the thought that you might actually be rejected by him."

Tammy would never have the balls to admit it, but they both knew that Ms. Cruz was right.

For the past several months, Tammy had already felt like she had been rejected, and she couldn't actually handle him confirming those emotions.

"Oh well," Tammy said as she slammed her laptop shut. "Life goes on either way. Anyway, I'm just going to finish my work somewhere else because, for some strange reason, I'm having a problem concentrating now," she said sarcastically.

"Oh please, drowning yourself in your work is not going to fix your problems. You and Patrick broke up, and you were still hurt about it when your father was murdered. You've had to take over all of your dad's stuff while managing your own business. You work every day for at least 16 hours a day. If you don't take care of yourself first, everything is going to collapse right in front of you. Because if you would slow down long enough, to be honest with yourself, you're not fixing or healing anything about your life. You're just finding ways to keep yourself busy. That's it."

"I don't have time to be stressing over a man who has other bitches stressing over him too. I've got the NYPD and the feds trying to extort me for more money than my father paid, work prices are going up, and one of my men brought his money short this week. On top of that, my distributor doesn't know when it's going to restock my most sold and sought-after lipsticks. I'm too damn stressed out already, and I'm not going to let a man add on to my problems. Regardless of how you feel about how I'm living my life, he would just be a distraction."

Tammy was aggravated, but Ms. Cruz had stayed silent for way too long. She knew Tammy well enough to know that Tammy was only working so hard to keep her mind off of her problems.

"Mi amor," Ms. Cruz said softly as she joined Tammy on the couch she was sitting on. "Have you forgotten that Patrick ran some of these same streets that your father did? He also has done this a lot longer than you. Even if you guys never see eye to eye on a romantic level again, why don't you just let him help you out until everything calms down?"

"I don't need his help. As a matter of fact," Tammy stated as she stood up, "I don't need anyone's help."

"Now, I know I taught you better than that. It is our job to look out for each other. I didn't say that you should sleep with him or even give him a chance to explain himself, but please give him a call. I'm sure it will help with your sanity and your business if you had a chance to bounce some ideas off of him."

***

Being in her father's apartment again for the first time since his death brought chills to her spine. Tammy had always bitched about wanting to have a set of keys to his house, but she never imagined the price she would have to pay to have them.

It was hard for her to sit and relax when every room was filled with some sort of memory from Patrick or her father.

Just when Tammy had decided to grab her bag and leave, the knock she had been waiting for occurred at the front door. She checked herself out again in the mirror before she opened it.

Tammy had coached herself several times while she was waiting to just remain calm, cool, and unaffected by him like she had been with so many other men. She didn't want to play herself with him again, and she knew that she was not over him. Every part of her still craved for him. She took one last deep breath before opening the door.

Regardless of how much she had prepped for this moment, nothing had prepared her the flood of emotions that hit her when she saw him standing in the doorway.

"Long time no see, but like always, you look nice," Patrick said as he took a moment to admire Tammy's beauty. "It's about time you finally called me."

"You say that confidently like you knew I was going to," Tammy huffed.

"I did because I knew you would do it eventually. Do you honestly think you could ever forget about the chemistry we had or what we mean to each other? I know you felt that shit too. I know I wasn't alone in my feelings."

"Ugh. Please stop," Tammy said flatly as she moved to the side to allow him in. "I called you over here to discuss business, nothing more and nothing less."

"So that's really it," he asked. "You're not even going to ask me any questions or give me a chance to explain anything to you? You're just going to blow off my feelings and go off of what someone else said, and it doesn't matter what I have to say about it? You're really going to be like this?"

"I'm glad to see that we are finally on the same page about something. The whole time we spent together, you always had to explain shit to me, and frankly, I'm just flat out tired of hearing your explanations.

I don't care to know your side of the story. I care that you're a businessman; I'm a businesswoman, and we have potential opportunities to make money together. That's it. Fuck all that other shit because it never profited me anything anyway."

"Fine," he said as he took a seat on the couch. "I have no choice but to respect what you want. There is no need to get your pretty panties in a bunch.

Anyway, I just knew you would eventually be wise enough to call me, so I already got a plan together."

"Wow," Tammy stated as she took a seat in her dad's favorite recliner. "I'm getting ready to get survival advice from a drug lord and thief. What has my life become?"

"You can label me whatever the hell you want to, but I know what I am. Clearly, my plans have been pretty good to me, but you don't have to find out for yourself if that would be too low for you, princess," he said in a sarcastic tone. "If you don't truly want my help, I could just see myself out."

"No. There is no need to do that, old man. As much as I don't want to admit it, your help would be really nice right now," Tammy confessed.

"I thought you'd see things my way. Anyway, there is a dealer back home who is making major moves. He used to work as your dad's right hand, so he's pretty pissed that you took his spot. He wants to get close to you and take all of this from you."

"How the hell do you know that," Tammy asked.

Patrick pulled out a sheet of paper from his pocket and placed it on the coffee table.

"On that sheet of paper is his business website. There you are going to find his e-mail. When you use the password that is also on that sheet of paper, you'll be able to log in to his e-mail and find out his master plan for yourself. All you have to do is use that to your advantage to be one step ahead of him at all times.

Tammy grabbed her laptop that happened to be sitting next to the sheet of paper and immediately looked it up.

When she was finally inside his mailbox, she was surprised at all of the e-mails he suggested that she look at.

"Who is this creep," Tammy asked as she stared at the screen in disbelief. "He knows where I eat, shop, and the names of the men I usually keep around me."

"His name is Brian Maverick, and he took over all of the territories your dad had in Boston. Now, he moves product for me, but he feels like because most of his clients are powerful, wealthy, and have a reputation to protect that he is untouchable.

Real talk, I hate that I have to deal with him, but because your father was killed the night he was supposed to re-up, he had no other choice but to come to me. Now that he knows about you, he thinks this could be his time to come up, and he has the army and collateral to try it. Not to mention, his friendships with some big names in the NYPD could explain all of the problems that you've been having with them niggas."

"Ok," Tammy started. "Now, I'm left with two issues. One, how do I know that you're really on my side. I mean, you and my dad ran in similar circles and ran the same kind of operation. Aren't you guys supposed to hate each other or be rivals or something? How am I supposed to know that this isn't your way of coming in like a knight in shining armor while trying to claim all of my dad's shit? Anyway, my next problem is that I have this information, and I do to do with it."

Patrick chuckled. "I love that you're so smart because you read all of those damn books, but they are the same reason why you have a messed up view on this game. Yes, we ran in similar circles, and we had similar business operations, but your dad is the man where I'm from. That's why no one was dumb enough to cross that man when he was alive. If your dad was still here, this Brian cat would have still been doing his shit quietly. Sadly, a lot of people seem to forget that part of what made him powerful was the connections that he maintained. Just because he is not here anymore does not mean people should be crossing you. That nigga is about to find out that lesson the hard way. That's why you don't need to worry about me. I do this shit because I still feel something for you, but I love my life too much to play against Delino Santiago, even if he isn't here to make a move himself. In regards to your other question, don't stress, beautiful. That's what I'm here for. I'm going to coach you through all of this.

Brian loves black women, and he knows you have something that he wants, so you already have an advantage on your hands. My sister, who has her doctorate in psychology and is my most trusted confidant, is going to come over and prepare you for this meeting that I'm planning for next week. You cannot give him any indication that you know what he's up to, and you definitely cannot let him think you're really running this show. He just cares about getting next to all of that money your dad left for you."

"It's disgusting what some people will do for a quick buck," Tammy snared.

"Yeah. I've seen people try to sell their own babies for a dime, but who knows what someone would do to try to get close to the money Delino left for you. Most people will never get the chance to see billions of dollars."

Tammy sat frozen. She didn't even know how to respond to his statement. She had heard rumors that her father left her a substantial amount of money, but she had never cared enough to ask. She knew her dad was a hard worker, but she was shocked to hear it so bluntly.

"Don't act so surprised. Your dad was a drug dealer, but he was also a smart-ass businessman. That man had hotels and restaurants in different states and countries. I heard that number maybe ten years ago. Who knows where it is now? Anyway, tomorrow you're going to sit down and meet with my sister. She is going to help coach you on exactly how to handle this, and she can hopefully clear a few things up so we can move past all of this."

They agreed to meet at their usual spot, so the meeting wouldn't be awkward. Tammy walked into the small sports bar and sat at her regular seat.

Without asking her what she wanted, the bartender fixed her favorite drink of Remy and coke. Then, he placed it in front of her.

"Thanks love, but I wasn't planning on drinking today," Tammy responded as she took the small black straw and stirred her drink.

"Ms. Santiago, I know you usually drink after you've eaten, but the woman over there was adamant that she had to buy you a drink as soon as you arrived."

Tammy glanced in the direction that the bartender and owner, Ryan, had nodded his head in.

Tammy's heart sunk down to her feet when she made eye contact with the beautiful woman who smiled at her from across the bar. She watched the woman get up and sashay to grab a seat next to Tammy.

"Good afternoon, Tee," she spoke softly.

"Tee is a name reserved for close family and friends. You are neither. If you insist on speaking to me, then Ms. Santiago will work just fine," Tammy replied sternly. "Anyway, I'm really not in the mood for any of your shit, and I have a business meeting soon. I would appreciate it if you kept what you had to stay to yourself and left me the hell alone."

The woman was not surprised at Tammy's firm demand and evident attitude. Still, she was surprised at how classy she had remained through her anger.

"I like you, Ms. Santiago. You've got balls, brains, and beauty. I see why my brother acts the way he does with you."

Tammy sat there for a moment, completely puzzled, so the woman used that as her chance to continue.

"My name is Josie Bennett-Carter. I'm not Patrick's wife or mother of his children. I'm actually just his older sister."

Tammy had spent six months of her life trying to move on from the only man she had ever really loved because of the lies that this woman had personally said directly to her face.

Every day for six months, Tammy relived that painful memory of confronting the 'special woman' in Patrick's life that he had neglected to mention to her. Every time she thought of her, her face would turn red from the embarrassment of being played. Tammy also couldn't forget how ashamed she was as she had allowed a woman to threaten her life while all she could do was run away to hide the tears she forced back.

"What the fuck," Tammy yelled out as she slammed her drink down, causing some to spill over.

"Please calm down, Tammy. I mean, Ms. Santiago. You don't want anyone to overhear a woman in your position acting out, especially not off of any love shit."

Tammy knew she was right. If she had been in her right mind, she would have gotten up and left, but the anger she felt allowed her emotions to trump her logic.

There were only a few patrons in the bar, but Ryan knew who Tammy was to the streets now, and he thought it would be best to have everyone else clear out once he saw Tammy lose her cool. Because of the money Tammy spent in his establishment so frequently, he had allowed her to have free reign over the place.

"Fuck that and fuck you! Do you have any idea what the shit you pulled put me through?"

Tammy was livid. She was so hurt, angry, and confused that all she wanted to do was cry. It took everything in her to contain her composure because she refused to let Josie see her that weak ever again.

"I can't believe that I allowed myself to get caught up with you, your brother, and your sick childish games. I would actually appreciate it if you would both just leave me the fuck alone."

Tammy got up, chugged down the rest of her drink, and reached for her keys and red clutch purse when Josie reached out and grabbed her hand to stop her.

"Just let me explain. I know you're angry, but I can promise you that it's not what you think."

Tammy glared at her. "Get your hands off of me before I forget that you're actually Patrick's sister and whoop yo' ass," she roared, meaning every word.

Without any debate, Josie did just as Tammy had demanded.

Tammy turned to leave, and just as she was almost to the door, Patrick walked in.

"Tee, please sit down, and we can get this all straightened out," he said as he reached out to embrace her, which was something he rarely did. Tammy pulled away from him and spoke sternly. "Get out of my way."

"You're being dramatic, and you have no idea what's going on. Please just let Josie explain everything."

Tammy had already been fighting back the tears long enough. She just wanted to get out of there as fast as she could. She tried to move past him without saying anything else, and once again, he blocked her attempt to leave.

"Sit the fuck down," Patrick demanded. "If you don't want her to clear up the personal stuff, then she won't. But think about the business shit for a moment."

Tammy wasn't sure how long she could swallow the tears, and she was determined to get out of there before either of them could see just how much Tammy still cared about him.

"The only man who ever had any right to talk to me like that was buried six months ago, and he didn't even speak to me with this much bass in his voice. Get the fuck out of my way - *now*."

This time he did as she requested, and Tammy was relieved. With each step she took towards the door, the more tears she allowed to silently escape to cleanse her of all of the hurt and pain she had been holding in.

Once she had walked a few blocks away and was sure that they hadn't followed her, she allowed herself to finally be free of the tears she had been clenching onto since the day of her father's funeral. That was the last time she cried, and she thought she would never have another tear left inside of her. It had embarrassed Tammy to be so weak the first time and allow Ms. Cruz to see her that way, but this time was different. For the first time in her life, a man was able to stir up that kind of passion and emotion out of her.

Tammy stood there in a sea of people and felt so alone. She remembered Ms. Cruz's words that there was a time to cry, so she did. This time, however, she didn't care who saw her.

***

"What the fuck were you thinking," Jason screamed out as Tammy climbed in his all-black Chevy Tahoe. "Why did one of your runners have to call me and tell me that I needed to come check you because you were out here being soft as shit?"

One of Tammy's guys had seen her breakdown and called Jason to get him to help her out.

"Why don't you understand who the fuck you are now? It's bad enough that some of these men hate the idea of following orders from a broad without you being so vulnerable and emotional out here."

"Jason, I hear you, and I'm sorry. I was just -" she started to reply.

"Yeah, you will be fucking sorry," he interrupted. "Can you imagine what would happen if your employees and connects knew that you couldn't control your personal life, much less this organization? Some of these niggas have been waiting for a reason to come for your crown. Now, you just want to give it to them? To some of these niggas, they don't give a fuck about who your father was or the work he built up. All they see is an easy opportunity to sit in the seat your dad busted his ass for."

Tammy hadn't thought about that before. Now, she felt foolish for allowing her emotions to get the best of her. She was already dealing with the attitude of men who wanted to have her in any other position besides the one she was in. She couldn't fathom what would happen if the rest of the camp got wind of this.

Sensing her change in mood, Jason spoke softer this time. "I couldn't wait on you. I already gave the OK for the hit. It's been handled."

Tammy immediately felt relief knowing that she had nothing else to worry about. Then, a wave of guilt washed over her as she realized the young man's life had to end because of it. It was at that moment she said a silent prayer. Tammy prayed for his family. Then, she asked for strength and promised her father that she would never put his empire in that kind of situation over her vulnerability ever again.

They pulled up in front of the building that Tammy had once found comfort in, but this time her safe haven felt like her own personal torture chamber. She briefly imagined the walls of the apartment caving in on her. They seemed to be filled with the same sorrow Tammy's heart was filled with.

"I can't go up there," she said. "I don't think I could ever go back there."

Jason had known Tammy to be so strong, and it killed him to see her acting this way.

Even though he wasn't very emotional himself, he had developed quite the soft spot for her. "I'll have all of your things moved out tonight. Your father has a big ass, nice ass home in Boston if you're interested. All you have to do is say the word, and I'll have it all set up.

Without any hesitation, she responded, "Do it."

***

The car ride to Boston was peaceful and exactly what Tammy needed. She was silent most of the time because she was too busy going over all of the crazy events that had only occurred in a short time.

"He loves you even though he won't come out and say it," Jason said, finally breaking their silence. "You should reach out to him and hear him out."

Tammy sighed heavily. She had managed to cry more tears in 180 days than she ever had her entire life. Now that she had time to cool off, she desperately wanted to hear what he had to say, but she didn't want to make the first move. She also knew him well enough to know that he wasn't going to try again after he had made such a blatant attempt earlier.

"I think it's just too late now, Beast. I think it's time to just close that chapter of my life and move forward."

"You can't. Whether you want to believe it or not, you need Patrick right now. There is no way you can handle business here and in New York at the same time. Not to mention all of this drama that is going on with this clown Brian and all of the problems we've been having with the NYPD back home. Maybe he isn't the man you decide to be with, but you can at least use him and his muscle in the streets to help you get things back on track. As much as I hate to say it, you need him right now. And because he's really my boy, I can be honest and say that he needs you too."

"Well he's not going to reach out to me, and I'm definitely not going to reach out to him."

"You both are way too damn stubborn. I hate that shit about both of ya'll. What's why I didn't allow that to affect our flow. I told him that we had business to handle up here, so he caught a flight and is already at the house waiting.

***

Tammy felt a rush of nervousness as she walked up to the door.

She walked into the large, beautiful, and wonderfully decorated home and saw Patrick dozed off on the living room sofa. She walked over and quietly slipped off his Nike Air Max's and gently laid the plush blanket that was sitting on the large ottoman over him.

If she ever had any doubt before, that moment confirmed something she hated to admit - she was dangerously in love with Patrick Bennett. It didn't seem to matter what he did or said. He stirred up feelings and emotions out of her that she never knew she was capable of feeling.

Just as she had turned to leave the living room to tour the rest of the house, she heard him speak up with a soft, raspy voice.

"Come here, princess," Patrick said as he sat up on the couch.

This time she didn't object. Tammy was relieved that he seemed to want to be as close to her as she wanted to be to him.

She sat next to him on the large leather sectional, and he reached over and gently laid his hand on her thigh.

As they both sat there awkwardly somewhere in between love and misunderstanding, neither of them said a word, although there was so much that needed to be said.

After several moments of silence, Patrick spoke up first. "She really is just my sister. Your friend came poking around asking all kinds of personal questions about me, and she thought it would be best to get close to her to find out why she was so interested in me. That was the only reason she played that part. If I had known that you would have reacted that way, I would have just talked to you about it before my sister did what she did."

"If that's the case, then why did you let it get this far without telling me? You know how to make your point heard for everything else. I'm sure you could have figured out how to clear this up before now. Do you have any idea what this has been like for me for the last six months," she broke down and admitted to him.

"I've been trying to tell you, Tee, but remember you didn't want to hear it? You kept telling me how much you loved me, yet you let someone you didn't know and your fake friend come between us without hearing anything that I had to say. I may not know a lot about love and relationships, but I know that you can at least hear them out if you claim to care about someone.

Listen, I know I'm not the kind of man your father would have wanted for you. Shit, I love you enough to say that I would like you to have the type of man that would do all of the corny shit you deserve without you having to live like this. Maybe I'm just in too deep with this shit that I can't recondition my mind to be for you what you really need.

I'm not going to make you a bunch of promises, princess, but I will always keep it real with you. If you chose to do this life shit with me, just know that I'm not that nigga that will sweep you off of your feet. But I am the kind that will keep you on your toes."

Tammy felt a flood of emotions. More than anything, she felt foolish. She couldn't believe she had allowed a lie to keep them from each other for so long.

Tammy got up from her seat and sat in his lap. Then, she wrapped her arms around his neck and kissed him passionately. She had missed his touch and the warmth of his skin next to hers.

He lifted her up and softly laid her back on the couch. He fervidly kissed her neck as he lifted her dress up above her head.

Typically, sex between Tammy and Patrick was intense and super rough, but this time he handled Tammy very gently. He made love to her for hours, and when he was done, they ate and went back at it again.

***

My brother really cares about you," Josie told Tammy as they peacefully enjoyed lunch. "It's actually weird to watch him act like this," she chuckled.

For as long as Tammy had been dealing with Patrick, she knew he wasn't big on PDA, romance, or even affection. Shit, she had only ever heard him say he loved her once, so she had no idea what Josie could have been talking about.

"Well, if I should feel special, then I would hate to see how he treats everyone else."

"Oh boy," Josie started. "Patrick doesn't really trust women. In his mind, every woman he meets either wants his penis, product, or pennies, and he's not the type to just give out any of those.

His lack of trust is the reason for his inability to love, and you know you cannot have love where there is no trust. I can tell that he's really trying with you, and he's never done that before.

To my brother, wisdom is everything. He doesn't allow women to know where he lays his head at night or ever meet me. He feels like someone having that kind of information could help them understand his mind or figure out his moves.

When he gave me the rundown on this, I seriously thought it was just a joke. So, it surprised me to learn that he got all of the details on what this guy has planned, and he had a plan of his own."

Tammy was surprised and didn't know how to respond. She had always felt like he didn't care because he hardly ever showed it. She was finally starting to understand that he just showed his love for her differently.

"It's imperative that nosy Nancy has no idea that we met or are working together. Something about her just doesn't sit right with me, and I need to get to the bottom of this. She is a very hateful and envious person, so if you're not careful, this could be terrible for you."

Tammy had heard for years that she should cut Tanya off, but she had always hoped that Tanya would show the same loyalty she had given her. Even with all of the evidence beginning to mount against her, she felt like she might have reached out to Josie because she was just genuinely concerned. She decided to just drop that part of the conversation.

"You've worked with Jason and my father for a long time right," Tammy asked.

"I've been in this game longer than you've been alive. Your father will always have a special place in my heart.

He was quite the flirt," she said with a smirk. "But for a 'heartless lion,' he had a lot of love to give. Anyway, what made you ask that?"

"I need a huge favor," Tammy responded with much excitement. "What do you know about one of his business partners, Lorenzo?"

CHAPTER FOUR

Isabella rolled off of K.Y., and they were both drenched in sweat and absolutely exhausted. She grabbed the spliff she had on the nightstand and lit it.

K.Y. had been dodging his obvious attraction to Isabella because of his desire to get closer to Tammy. Still, if he had any idea how amazing in bed she was, he would have slept with her sooner.

"I take back all of my jokes about your dick," she said with a giggle as the smoke slowly escaped her mouth.

He laughed.

He wasn't sure if it was the way she swallowed him whole and everything that he released, or if it was the way she rode him without tiring, but he had a whole new attitude towards her now.

"I had no idea you were so skilled. I've never had a female ride my dick and tell me a whole story at the same damn time," he responded as he was exhaling the smoke from the spliff she had just passed him.

She laughed.

It had been years since K.Y. had been inside of a woman, and it was the first time he had sex with someone who knew what she liked and exactly how she wanted it. He liked that, and just the thought of going another round was enough to get him hard again.

She noticed his excitement growing, so she grabbed his member in her hand.

"You haven't seen anything yet, papi," she purred in his ear as she began jacking him off. "However, we need to stay focused. Our purpose is revenge, and we're going to get it because she deserves to pay for what she's done to us.

Get dressed, so I can have Josie come by and help me explain everything you need to know about her. That way, we'll both finally have her exactly where we want her.

Once this is done, I'm going to show you all of the things I held back today."

Without any hesitation, he got up and did exactly as she had just suggested.

"Oh," she exclaimed as he was about to head to the bathroom. "The girl who lives in your mom's crib asked me to give this to you."

She handed him a white envelope with his name scribbled on the front. Without opening it, he knew exactly who it was from, just from the handwriting.

He hesitated to open it because he had no idea what would be inside after all of this time. After a few moments of debating on if he should just throw the thing away and pretend that he never saw it, he decided to open it with hopes he would finally get answers to questions that had been haunting him for years.

My dear Kyle,

I know it's been a while, but I was caught up in stuff you would never be able to understand. I can't stay here very long, but I need to see you while I'm still in town.

Love always,
Mommy

CHAPTER FIVE

"Let me get this straight," Jason started, obviously confused. "Instead of trying to come up with a plan on how to handle this clown Brian, you would rather play matchmaker," he asked Tammy.

"Yes, Jason, because this isn't just any love connection. We are going to be reuniting two people who really love each other. Don't you get that?

Ma is going to be so excited when I put my plan in motion," she said with a smile. "I've thought about every last little detail, and this plan is foolproof.

There is a rapper out in Orlando that goes by the name Skeme. According to my source, he is going to be the one to lead me to Lorenzo."

"So why are you telling me all of this," he asked, again clearly confused.

"Because you're going to be my plug. I already rented out a studio out there, and I need him to trust you so that he'll trust me enough to give me what I need.

I'll be in Boston playing the role of a woman who handles business and is living off of her father's inheritance. I trust you enough to know that the men you've trained will be able to do their job while I do that. Patrick is going to keep things moving for me in New York while I'm traveling back and forth."

"How the hell do you plan on getting someone to give you the information you want about a man who had to fake his own death to escape the feds?"

"With drugs and free studio time, duh," Tammy said in a matter-of-fact tone. "I don't care how much it costs us, but you find a reliable plug with good product that he wants, and you make sure you keep him there until I'm able to get down there. I know we could just give him the shit we have, but we have to make it look more reliable with you having connections out there."

Realizing her mind was made up and seeing that she already had the plan in motion, he knew there was no way of getting out of this one.

"When do I leave," he asked.

***

Although Jason was initially hesitant to follow Tammy's orders, her plan was moving smoothly.

In the time that he had been in Orlando, Jason managed to land a connect with good product and develop a good relationship with the rapper Tammy wanted him to get in good with. Luckily for him, Skeme was a talented rapper so in the time that he had been working as a producer, he was finally starting to see it pay off financially. In fact, he was making so much legal money that he began to seriously consider retiring instead of just joking about it.

He knew that today was going to be the day that Tammy and Patrick set Brian up for his plot to take Tammy's throne. He was suddenly beginning to get a little nervous about not being able to be there to protect them.

He knew Tammy well enough that he knew she could handle herself, but he knew firsthand that something unplanned could always occur. The night Delino died was a perfect example of that.

Delino didn't tell anyone other than Jason that he had planned to get away for the night to be with his only daughter. Although most of Lino's employees had no idea of his whereabouts, Jason was all on it.

After Tammy and Lino enjoyed a nice quiet evening together, he pulled Lino aside before leaving the restaurant with Tammy.

"I've already got eyes on Tee," Jason declared as he tried to convince Lino to take his usual car that had all of the protection he would need.

"I'm a grown man," Lino stated confidently. "These thugs won't fuck with me, and neither will the police. I just need to be off of the radar for a moment. All of this sentimental shit ain't good for someone like me," he joked as he tried to lighten the mood.

Despite his gut feeling to stay with Lino, he was the boss, so Jason had to do what he said. Once he was sure that Tammy was in the car with the men who would protect her, Jason decided to hang out across the street to discretely watch Lino anyway. Lino usually knew the importance of having muscle around him in case anything popped off. Jason didn't want to ignore the gut feeling he had that something terrible was about to happen.

As soon as he saw Lino walk down the block and turn right, he began slowly walking in his direction. He was halfway down the block when he heard three gunshots. He immediately took off in the direction he just saw Lino take.

Once he saw the self-proclaimed heartless lion lying on the cement, he managed to run even faster than he had moments before. As soon as he made it to him, he realized that all three shots had managed to hit their intended target. He pulled out his phone and dialed 911.

"What the fuck are you doing here," Lino asked softly. "You should be with Tee. If anything happens to her, I'll -,"

"I'd die before I let something happen to her," Jason responded sincerely.

"Good. Mad niggas out here, and none of these niggas are gonna talk. You know that right," Lino asked Jason accepting that his death may never be avenged.

"Nah," Jason said. "We're gonna get the mothafucker that did this to you. Give me a name. Tell me what you saw."

"I didn't see who did it, but I did see that nigga Derrick around here. He has to know something," Lino managed to say before he violently started coughing up blood.

Knowing he was near death, he changed the direction of his conversation.

"Just protect my baby, or I'll come back and kill you my damn self. I thought I would have had more time to prepare her for what she's about to take over, but I trust you'll do your part. Don't let me down nigga."

Reminiscing on Lino's final moments always filled Jason's heart with regret. He knew he should have stuck with his gut feeling and not let him out of his sight. Still, he was having a hard time letting go of the remorse and guilt – mainly because he never avenged his death like he promised.

Now that he was feeling completely uninspired, he just sat motionless in front of his keyboard as he anxiously awaited a text that

Tammy was ok and everything had gone smoothly. Unexpectedly, a buzz from his front door broke him out of his funk.

Jason was surprised to see that of all people, Derrick would be the face that showed up on his surveillance video.

After Delino's death, Derrick basically fell off the face of the earth. No one knew his whereabouts, and he stopped coming around to re-up on product.

Jason didn't have enough proof to take anything to Tammy, so he wanted to wait before initiating a full-out manhunt. He knew her well enough to know that Tammy would have found some way to blame herself if she knew that Derrick had anything to do with her father's death.

He buzzed him in after he pulled out his pistol and made sure it was loaded.

He anxiously waited for Derrick to follow the directions that would lead him to the studio he was sitting in. Still, on the outside, he looked just as calm and relaxed as he always was. Because Jason never trusted Derrick, he got up to open the door, so he wouldn't have any way of surprising him. Then, he sat back down with his pistol in clear view on his lap.

As soon as Derrick could see a clear view of Jason, he immediately started speaking,

"Look, man, I know it's been a minute since you last saw me. I also know that you talked to Lino the night of his death, and I know he saw me there, but I can promise you that I had nothing to do with it."

"Fuck that," Jason responded as he stood up and began making his way to Derrick while his gun was pointed in that direction. "An innocent man would have no reason to just fall off the face of the earth. Strip down right now. I need to know you aren't holding heat or a wire."

Without hesitation, Derrick did as he was told. He took off everything, only leaving his underwear on to show Jason that he wasn't hiding anything from him.

"Now that you see I'm not holding anything, can I put my clothes on and tell you why I'm here?"

"Nah nigga. Start talking before I start shooting just off of my assumptions of your actions."

"Look, man, the only reason I ran was because the biggest drug dealer on the east side had died, and I was the last face he probably recognized before it happened. I swear I didn't have shit to do with his murder, but I finally have information on the person who did it. That's the only reason why I'm here."

For some reason, Jason believed what he said, so he lowered his weapon and nodded at Derrick's clothes to let him know it was cool to put them back on. After he got dressed, he took a seat on the couch and began explaining what he knew.

"The night Lino died, I had a drug deal with a broad that always bought large orders. The only thing I knew about her was that she was from out of town. I didn't know her name or anything about her. All I knew was that her orders got larger every time I served her, and I needed the money.

The night Lino died, she offered to buy the rest of the product that I had been holding. That wasn't weird to me because she had done that several times, but that time she was obviously high and paranoid. The broad kept asking me if I was the police or if I knew who had her kids. I just kept telling the bitch to give me the money because I wanted to get away from her as fast as I could. Still, she said she wouldn't do it until she saw the product because that was the only way she would believe me. Now, you know I had been dealing for a lil while, so the last thing I wanted to do was show a paranoid broad what I was holding. When I wouldn't show her what I had, she pulled out her piece and pointed it at me."

Derrick paused for a moment as he stared off, almost reliving the final moments before Lino was murdered.

"Yeah, I grew up in the streets, but nothing can ever prepare you for that moment that might be your last. I just stood there frozen, so when I made eye contact with Lino... I...I don't know. I'm sure my eyes got wide or something, but the broad turned around, and when she shot her first shot, I just took off. I couldn't chance the police finding me with what I had on me or her turning around to hit me next."

Derrick hung his head low and was silent for a few moments before he started speaking again.

"I know I probably just came off as some entitled hood nigga, but I truly cared for Tammy. I couldn't face her or anyone on her team until I had answers for her. A big part of me feels like even though I didn't pull the trigger that it was still my fault. If I would have just listened to my gut instinct and decided not to serve her, maybe Lino could have still been alive today."

"Look," Jason said to try to break the eerie silence. "I wasn't a fan of you only because of the love and genuine concern I had for Tammy, but you don't need to live with the guilt. If you didn't pull the trigger, it's not your fault. Honestly, it's a part of this game we signed up to play," Jason was shocked at the stuff coming out of his mouth. He hoped that what he was saying would help Derrick because, for some reason, he couldn't believe a word he was saying for himself. "No one ever plans to lose their king when they sit down to play chess, but when we agreed to play, we knew that it was a possibility it could happen; that's what happened with you. That's why Lino used to always say, 'how much would you risk if what you lost you had to charge it to the game.' He understood that at some point everyone was going to lose. You just have to accept that before you decide to be a player in the game."

"For real, I really appreciate you saying that shit," Derrick responded. "It's been really hard living with this, but it fueled me to get more information on the broad that I was serving because a part of me refused to just leave it alone."

"You got a name," Jason asked as he sat up in his chair.

"Sasha Cole."

CHAPTER SIX

"You really expect me to believe that my mother *killed* Tammy's father? You sound crazy right now."

After they finished a few more rounds, Isabella and K.Y. got dressed so they could meet at Josie's office so she could fill in some of the blanks.

"I know my mom has done some fucked up shit, but I've never known my mom to be a killer. Before she got hooked on that shit, she used to take care of people. This doesn't make any sense, and ya'll better make it make sense before I take Tammy's advice and leave you birds alone."

"You have every right to be upset," Josie said, finally speaking up. "It's a lot to take in, and it's a lot to accept, but I'm only here to help fill in the gaps."

"So, if Tammy really believes that my mother killed her dad, then why is my mom not dead?"

"Tammy was getting close to you in hopes of locating your mother. The reason she had you move out was so she could have an inside man in the house in case your mother ever returned."

"Then why the fuck did this bitch just bring me a letter from my mom? How do I know that you two aren't a part of this in some way? I mean, I met you guys through her."

"Kyle," Josie said in a sweet and loving tone. "I can tell you are really triggered by what we are saying here, and I can promise you that I am on your side. The only way you will get the answers you are honestly hoping for is if we continue this with an open mind.

I hear everything you are saying, and in some ways, it doesn't make sense. Tammy could have killed you a long time ago, yet here we are. One thing you should know about Tee, if you don't already know is that she does everything meticulously. There is a reason why you both are still breathing.

For years, no one knew how to find your mom. She was so strung out that shit that we never really had any leads to prove she was even alive. That's why Tammy went in search of you, Kenya, and Kennan."

"Hold the fuck up," K.Y. spat as he stood to his feet. "Tammy knows where my siblings are?"

Not wanting to be the bearer of bad news, Josie just hung her head low.

"Yes," Isabella shouted. "That bitch knows where your twin siblings are. In fact, she has both of those niggas on her payroll right now."

Unlike Josie, Isabella seemed to enjoy upsetting K.Y. with the knowledge she was holding in.

"Okay," Josie spoke up, trying to restore peace. "Let's have a seat, and I can go into more detail about that information."

"Fuck that," K.Y. shouted. "We are talking about my baby siblings that I haven't seen in years. You mean to tell me that I confided in Tammy about the guilt I had about not knowing where they were, and she knew all of this all along?"

Everyone in the room was silent as they gave him a moment to process the rollercoaster of emotions that he was feeling.

"I told Tammy things that I've never told anyone, and she used all of that information against me? When I got emotional with her about my family, why wouldn't she tell me that she knew about them? I stayed in that house, hoping they would return, and she knew that. Why? Why wouldn't she tell me? This doesn't make any sense. I mean, I understand her need for revenge. I'm sorry about the death of her father, but I never did shit to her. I don't deserve any of this shit. What the fuck?"

K.Y. took a deep breath and finally sat back down. Josie was the first one to break the silence.

"I knew this conversation was going to be hard, but I really didn't expect that I would be so hurt by your pain also. I'm so sorry that you are finding out this way, and I really just want to help you understand." Josie reached across the table to grab his hand. To her surprise, he let her.

"Wait one fucking minute," Isabella chimed in. "We aren't here for all of this emotional shit. We are here to give this nigga the facts so we can get revenge. Tell his ass the rest of the story so we can get to the best part of this fucking nightmare."

"Shut the fuck up," Josie screamed. "I've been trying to just let you be the boss and do this your way, but you are really impossible to work with. I see why Tammy cut your ass off."

Sensing that Isabella was about to snap, Josie made sure to make her point clear.

"In case you forgot bitch, I'm the closest person to Patrick and Tammy. You don't know where they are or how to reach them, which is why you need me. So, if you want that information, you're going to shut the fuck up. Am I clear?"

Isabella nodded, but not before rolling her eyes first.

"Truthfully, there is a lot going on. Parts of the story señora bitchy over here doesn't even know, and that's the only reason why she's here. Homegirl is so offended that for years Tammy was her only friend, and now Tammy doesn't want shit to do with her.

How does it feel knowing that even when you were a snake in her grass, you still didn't get all of the dirt and information that she was hiding from you - bitch," Josie spat.

"Aight, ladies," K.Y interjected. "Look, the real reason I did all of this is because I wanted information on Skeme. I wanted to know if he was a part of why she wanted nothing to do with me, but I'm clearly missing a lot of pieces that go with this puzzle. I need to know everything. I'm willing to listen with a more open mind, but can we pour another drink first?"

"I know it's not easy to hear all of this, and it's probably going to get more confusing before you can process it all," Josie said as she poured them another round. "But Skeme was not a factor. He was just a pawn to get her to a man she desperately wanted to find. As a favor, she asked me to locate him, so I did. That's the main reason Jason was down here. Then, when the truth came out about your mom having a hand in her father's death, she wanted revenge.

The real reason why you are still here is because Tammy fell in love with you. Did she do some fucked up shit along the way? Yes, and it's because she wanted to really hurt you and your family, but I don't think she expected to fall in love with you during the process.

33

That day you were robbed in front of Jason's studio was supposed to be your last. Patrick thought Tammy was losing sight of the mission, so he kept interjecting. He felt like since no one could even prove your mother was alive that the best bet was to take you out. As soon as Tammy found out what was happening, she immediately went to your rescue. She took you on that vacation not to keep you from retaliating but because she knew you had a price on your head. Once she was sure that the streets knew your bounty was off, she allowed things to go business as usual.

Although Tammy had been in the game for a few years before meeting you, she had never personally had blood on her hands. Yeah, she had people killed, but eventually, you accept that as just a part of the game you're playing. Once she saw others take their last breath because of her hands, she wasn't quite the same after that."

"Tammy? A killer? I don't believe it," K.Y. spoke up.

"What happened to having an open mind," Josie chuckled while she poured them another drink.

"After Tammy found you that day, she moved you into her space to keep a closer eye on you. She had no idea that Patrick had the apartment bugged, and that's why he robbed you guys the night you proposed to her the first time.

When she left town after that, she planned to just confront him, but instead, her whole life changed.

CHAPTER SEVEN

"I'm not just one of your business partners," Tammy shouted. "I have emotional and physical needs too!"

Patrick never bothered to look up from his keyboard and just kept working.

"Hello! Do you hear a thing I'm saying here," Tammy's voice could be heard throughout his large condo. "Why is it that a man I've barely known wants to marry me, but a man that I've been with for years can't even give me two fucking minutes of his time? I deserve and *need* love and affection."

"Yeah, well, I *need* to get this done, so I *need* you to be quiet," he responded back emotionless. "Oh, and I *need* you to back away from this mission too. Clearly, you're going soft, and you've forgotten why you're dealing with him in the first place. Just look at what I had to do. Don't you think I have better things to do than to save you from you? Since we are so focused on our needs right now, I *need* you to get refocused." Without missing a beat, he continued typing.

Tammy grabbed her purse, glasses, and keys off the kitchen counter and headed towards the door.

"I guess the only thing obvious here is that we both just *need* two different things," Tammy stated, hoping that he would hear the desperation in her voice to save their struggling relationship.

"I guess so," Patrick responded.

***

"He just doesn't get it, ma. We've technically been together for years, but I honestly don't know what we are really doing. We don't live together or talk about the future. Can you believe this nigga told me the other day that I'm not the 'wedding type?' What does that even mean, and why does he feel like that's not what I really want? I guess I'm just starting to feel like he will never get it. I hate to admit that I feel like I'm only wasting my time at this point."

"Mi amor," Ms. Cruz said as she joined Tammy on the couch. "When summer is over, do you fret over it, or do you just prepare yourself for the next season that is coming?"

"Well, obviously, I prepare to show off all of my jackets and boots, but what does that have to do with this?"

"God puts some people in your life only for a season. Some seasons maybe a little longer than others, but you shouldn't cry or stress over something that you can't go back and change.

You're still young, and if you and Patrick don't want the same things out of life, you have to do what will bring happiness for you now. If the two of you are meant to be together, then no amount of distance or time is going to keep you two apart.

Just look, after all of this time, I'm going to see my darling Lorenzo," she said with a smile a mile wide.

"After all of these years, I finally get a chance to be with him again. I never thought I'd see the day."

Ms. Cruz wrapped her arms around Tammy and hugged her tightly.

"I'll never be able to repay you for the joy you've brought my life. It's been a pleasure just watching you grow, but now you've brought me back the only man I've ever loved. In less than 24 hours, I will be in the arms of my one true love.

Thank you, mi amor."

***

Tammy tried to mind her own business, but with all of the stories of the infamous Lorenzo, Tammy just had to meet him.

She showed up at Ms. Cruz's house a little before he was supposed to arrive and was surprised when she didn't find her out on the stoop. She eagerly ran up the stairs and used her key just like she always did.

"Hey, ma! I'm here to finally meet this man I've heard so much about, so if you're naked, put some clothes on," she called through the apartment jokingly.

There was no response.

Ms. Cruz never left the house without telling Tammy first, and the house didn't smell like freshly cooked food. While it was weird, Tammy tried not to think anything about it since today was supposed to be an extra special day.

Tammy spent a few minutes searching through the small apartment to find her. When her search came up empty, she decided to just have a seat on the couch and wait for her to return.

She probably had to get the cat waxed before her man got here and just didn't want me to know or maybe he picked her up early, Tammy thought to herself.

Not too long after that thought crossed her mind, there was a knock at the door.

Tammy opened the door and stood face-to-face with the man she had heard so many wonderful things about. She knew it was him because Ms. Cruz had done such a great job of describing him. He was gorgeous even in his old age, so it was no wonder Ms. Cruz was so taken with him.

"Good afternoon. Is Estrella in," he asked with a slight accent that she couldn't quite make out.

Tammy stepped aside to allow him in.

"No," she responded. "I'm honestly not sure where my grandmother ran off too, but I'm sure she'll be returning soon. I've heard so many wonderful things about you. I'm so happy to finally meet you!"

"Same here," he said as he walked into the apartment. "I really loved your father like a brother, so I'm glad his legacy gets to live on through you.

Oh, these are for your grandmother."

The flowers he handed her were gorgeous.

"These are so beautiful. Let me go put them in some water."

Tammy walked over to the small oak table that Ms. Cruz kept her vases. Once she bent down to get one from under the cabinet, she saw Ms. Cruz's keys.

"When was the last time you talked to my grandmother," Tammy asked as panic began to set in.

"I spoke with her yesterday morning to confirm our date. Is everything alright?"

"No," she responded frankly. "At first, I thought my grandmother was just careless and forgot to tell me that she ran out, but I just found her keys, so I know something is definitely not right."

Lorenzo got up for his seat on the couch. "I know you're still new to this kid, but you've got to pay attention to things like this more closely and with more urgency. Remember the game you're playing.

Now, when was the last time you saw her."

"I was here with her last night. Let me call my men who were on duty to see if they know where she is."

"No," he said sternly. "You're the boss, so do not give them time to concoct a lie. We're going to re-check this apartment thinking like an enemy, and then afterward, we are just going to surprise them."

They checked every square inch of her apartment to no avail.

Feeling defeated, they both took a seat at her kitchen table.

"What does that note on the fridge say," Lorenzo asked.

Tammy got up and read the letter she never noticed before.

To My Sweet Tee,

I had no idea that you were so cold, but you also had no idea that I was colder. Now, thanks to you, your grandmother is the coldest.

Enjoy my product and my money because now we're even.

Muah

xoxo

Tammy opened the stainless-steel fridge doors to find the woman who helped mold her into the person she was chopped up in small pieces in her own freezer.

She stood there emotionless.

She couldn't even bring herself to cry as the anger budding up inside of her began to take over.

"That motherfucker Brian is going to pay for this," she screamed out. "And the two motherfuckers that didn't do what I paid them to do are going to die tonight!"

She pulled out her phone and was about to dial Jason's number when Lorenzo slapped her phone out of her hands.

"What are you thinking? Do you have any idea what kind of problems you could be asking for? In case you haven't figured it out, you are now a drug lord and a target for every hungry man on these streets. If you get caught in a house with a dead body and millions in cash, you are going to rot underneath the jail or get extorted for a shit load of money.

Turn that phone off now and don't you turn it on or make another call until you are long gone from here. Oh, and make sure you take that note with you and trash it.

If anyone asks you, you were here with her today. Make sure you wait at least two days and then send the police over here to do a wellness check on her. This will give you time to handle your business and get far away from this place."

Despite her current circumstances, Tammy was glad that he was around to help her. Even though every part of her just wanted to hear her grandmother's voice or laugh or to see her smile one last time, she couldn't bring herself to tears.

Then, it hit her.

"What do you mean when you mentioned a house with millions of dollars in it? I paid everything for her because she didn't really have any."

Lorenzo fell into a fit of laughter.

"That's my baby," he chuckled. "Estrella was once poor, so she knows how to live on very little. I know that with as frugal as she was, there is no way she spent a fraction of that money we made together. If I know her as much as I knew her, that money is buried in the floor under her bed."

Tammy went over to her room and pulled out a pair of leather gloves, and began moving furniture to move the bed.

"Now you're thinking, kid." Lorenzo pulled out his own pair of gloves and began to help.

"Wait a minute," Tammy said as she stopped to face Lorenzo. "I carry a pair of gloves because I know I'm still in a position to get my hands dirty. You've been out for a while, so why do you still carry a pair with you?"

"You'll find out one day that some habits are hard to break. Yes, I have been out of the game for decades, but it's almost impossible to retrain your mind afterward. I bet if you look in your grandmother's purse, she'll probably have some in there too."

"She said it was because her hands would get cold easily."

Again, Lorenzo laughed at the idea of how well he still knew the love of his life.

Once they got the bed moved and carpet up, Tammy stared on in amazement at the safe in the bottom of the floor. She tried Ms. Cruz's birthday, debit pin, and her lucky numbers, but she just couldn't get in.

"Let me try," he suggested.

Tammy moved aside and was surprised when she noticed that he got it right on the first try.

"She always used our anniversary for really important things. Even now, she's still so predictable.

I honestly should have known that she would have still been here," he said as he took a seat on the floor. "I would have come back for her sooner if I knew.

Between me and you kid, I never loved anyone else but Estrella. I knew I wasn't going to find another woman like her, so I didn't even try. When it's my time to go, I'll have no one to leave all of my stuff to because the only person I could ever build with wasn't by my side."

Obviously, he was hurt, but like Tee, he had reconditioned himself to not show just how much pain he was really feeling inside.

"My grandmother felt the exact same way about you," Tammy responded as she managed to muster a small smile. "She always told the best stories about you, and when she did, it made her so happy. It was like she relived those precious moments every time she mentioned her 'sweet Lorenzo.'

As you know, I'm not biologically her grandchild because she never had any kids. Because of the way she still loved you, it would have been unfair to any man that would have ever tried to get into her heart."

They both sat there in silence for several moments before the suspense of the contents of the safe took over Tammy.

Once she laid eyes on the money, Tammy was convinced that there was easily a million dollars in there. She also found a small red notebook and a picture of her and Lorenzo in their prime.

"I can't believe she still had this," he said in amazement as he picked up the picture and notebook.

Tammy watched on as he lovingly ran his hand over her grandmother's picture.

"This journal is full of our poems and thoughts. Whenever we would be on different missions or opposite sides of the world, we would share our love through words and then mail it to each other."

He flipped through it and noticed an entry he never saw before.

My Sweet & Precious Lorenzo,
Missing you hurts
No matter how much I try, I can't seem to forget how smooth your skin was next to mine or how your kiss was as sweet as you are.
I'll never love another man, so I'll never even try.
My heart is yours until you come to have it again.
Te amo
Right under her signature was a perfect kiss with the red lipstick he

used to love to see her in.

He closed the journal, got up, and turned to leave the room. He moved quickly, but not fast enough to hide the tears that had escaped from his eyes.

***

"My two favorite employees. What's going on, guys?" It took everything in Tammy to not attack them right where they were standing, but she knew she couldn't afford to let her emotions overtake her at that moment.

"Nothing, boss lady, we were actually just about to head upstairs to check on your grandmother again," Devin responded.

"Oh, that won't be necessary. I'm going to give you two an opportunity to *die* for. Are you guys interested?"

"Hell yeah," they replied in unison.

"I'm going to give you an address. Do not write it down. Do not tell anyone, and most importantly, do not be late."

***

"What the fuck were you bums doing while my grandmother was murdered and dismembered," Tammy asked as she slapped Devin with the butt of her gun for what felt to him to be the hundredth time.

The boys had done exactly as directed and made sure not to be a second late. Once they got to the address she gave them, Tammy had them taken to an abandoned warehouse where they were placed in chairs with their arms and legs placed in shackles. She had them tied to the chair with duct tape over their mouth.

Tammy had been questioning and violently beating them for over an hour, and she was beginning to tire from it.

She put one in the head of her 9mm.

"The motherfucker who doesn't tell me what I want to hear is about to die. I've been asking questions, and now no one saw anything when I've been overpaying you guys because of the importance of this job. You two bastards literally had one fucking job, and that was to protect my grandmother. I had given you an entire team to your disposal along with more arsenal than the U.S. fucking army, so what the fuck happened?" Tammy gently placed her gun over Devin's face and let the coolness from the steel touch the sweat and blood dripping down his skin.

She knew that if any of them was going to crack, it was going to be him, so she decided to use that to her advantage.

She placed the loaded gun next to his temple and pressed it tightly against his skin.

"What the fuck was Junior doing Devin," she asked firmly, changing her demeanor. "If I ask again, I'm just going to shoot your brains out and send them to your mother. Please do not test me."

Not wanting to call her bluff, he finally cracked. "He was fucking Raquel under the stairwell," he finally spoke up.

"Really? You honestly expect me to believe that limp dick, minute man Junior was fucking that broad long enough for someone to dismember my grandmother and then clean up the entire apartment? Do I look that stupid to you?"

"I swear," he pleaded. "They had sex under the stairwell until her homegirl showed up. Then, they found a vacant apartment....and we all went in there to smoke and chill. It was a quiet night. We knew she was asleep already, and we just weren't thinking."

Tammy turned her attention and anger to Junior.

"You were screwing some dusty broad on my time? Don't I pay you well? Don't I make sure that you're able to provide nicely for your family? Didn't I make it easy by making sure you were never on shift for more than six hours? I pay you more in a month than most people make in a year, and all I was asking for was six hours of your undivided attention – a day. Are you really that thirsty that you couldn't wait six hours to smash this chick?

When I hired you, I remember that I told you I was putting my heart in your hands. Do you remember that, Junior?"

Junior nodded.

"Good. That means you remember the promise I made to you on what I would do if anything were to happen to her."

Tammy raised her gun.

"Please Tee. Don't hurt me. I'm sorry I..."

"Shut up," she snapped before pulling the trigger and shooting one fatal shot between his eyes.

His body went limp faster than she would have imagined, and she wasn't prepared for the amount of blood spatter that flew out everywhere. Almost in a trance, Tammy stared in disbelief. While she had always threatened to kill anyone who crossed her, she never thought that she would be the one to do it herself.

She didn't feel the power she imagined one would feel when they ended someone else's life. Getting revenge on the man who was partially responsible for her grandmother's murder didn't make her feel any better. Instead, it scared her. Her mind raced to the fact that a little girl just lost her father to this game, just like she did. How would she ever be able to look his family in the eyes after what she just did? Knowing that she was just as cruel as Brian, she suddenly felt powerless. How had she let this game turn her into the things she despised the most? Now, she was a *murderer* on top of everything else.

"Tee," Patrick called out bringing her back to reality.

For the first time since they all walked in the room, she remembered that they weren't alone. She looked up to see Patrick, Jason, and Lorenzo watching on. Then, she looked back down at the mess she created.

"You said you wanted to be the one to do this, so finish it," Patrick said sternly.

"I can't," she stated softly as she hung her head low and began crying. "This isn't who I want to be. I'm not a fucking murderer. I never asked for none of this shit, yo.

I didn't want to take over my father's dynasty. I didn't want to rob that nigga in the first place. Shit, I never knew him or had issues with him. I was just trying to protect something I didn't want in the first place. I never asked for none of this shit. Now, I've lost the only human on this Earth who really held me down, and I'm just supposed to act like this is business as usual? I can't fucking do this."

"No one ever grows up wanting to be a killer," Lorenzo chimed in. "In this game, it's either kill or be killed. If you let that kid walk out of here, you'll spend the rest of your life looking over your shoulder. He could walk out of here and go straight to the feds or come back to retaliate on his own.

I don't know if this helps or not, but the first one is always the hardest. As difficult as this is right now, you can't let him walk out of here. He's seen and heard way too much. Trust me, it's not going to make you feel any less guilty if one of us pulls that trigger."

She knew he was right.

"Tammy," Devin said, finally speaking up. "I promise I won't say a thing. I got kids, man. I wasn't even really friends with that nigga like that. I'm not going to tell anyone anything. Let me just take my family and get out of here. Please..."

She couldn't stand to hear him beg anymore. At that moment, she wondered if her grandmother had begged for her life or if she just took it like the gangsta' she knew her to be.

"I'm sorry," she whispered before emptying the rest of the clip into his body.

CHAPTER EIGHT

"I need another shot," K.Y. said, breaking their awkward silence. "This is a lot of shit to take in."

"Are you sure," Josie asked as she began to pour another round. "You look pretty fucked up already."

"Let my nigga get his drink on," Isabella chimed in. "This is the least we can do since we all fucked his life up."

"Speak for yourself," Josie retorted. "I was never part of the plan to take him down. You were. As a matter of fact, even after Tammy tried to leave this all alone, you refused to. If anything, you're the one who seems to enjoy tormenting him at this point."

"Ya'll really gonna talk about a nigga like I'm not sitting here? Just pour me another shot so we can get the rest of this information."

"Bitch," Isabella spoke up. "You are just a 'yes woman' that does what the fuck she is told. Unlike you, I'm not OK with doing whatever someone tells me to. I like to know what's going on and why. You're just as guilty in all of this shit, so you better relax before I slap the fuck outta you."

Josie immediately stood to her feet. "Do it then, bitch. You talk a lot of shit, so let's see if you're really about that action."

Isabella stood up ready to pop off, but K.Y was faster in breaking up their altercation.

"Yo, what the fuck is wrong with ya'll. I'll never get the shit I'm looking for if ya'll continue to act like this. Isabella, why don't you just wait for me in the car."

"Fuck that. I want the address too. You're not the only one who wants revenge."

"I get it, but at this pace, we ain't getting nowhere. I'll give you a chance to earn the address later," he seductively implied as he grabbed her hand to usher her to the door.

"I want that fucking address nigga, and I'm not fucking playing with you. You better keep your word," she whispered as she grabbed the keys from him.

"I'm trying to get some more of that ass tonight, so let me get this for us real quick. I got you."

Without any more hesitation, Isabella smiled and headed for the car.

Josie chuckled.

"What's so funny?"

"Everything about that just reminded me of Tammy. It's crazy how much she rubbed off on you."

"Please don't remind me," he said as he took his seat back at the table. "It's like I want to just get her out of my head, but a big part of me believes we had some real shit at times. I just don't know what to believe anymore."

"Look, my real position in this organization is my brains. I have my doctorates in psychology, so they keep me around to figure people out for them."

"Get the fuck outta here," he chuckled. "Now, you're just telling me anything."

"Seriously, between you and me, the only reason I'm around Isabella now is because Tammy isn't ready to let her go for some reason. I keep hinting that she is cut off by Tammy, but unfortunately, that isn't the truth. My brother has me around her to hopefully have some insight into what she may be planning for revenge. You know, it's the idea of keeping your enemies closer to you. Tammy, on the other hand, has me around her because I think a part of her wants everyone to be wrong about her. Tammy's life has changed so much in such a short time that she feels a sense of normalcy around Isabella, or Tanya as she has always called her, even though she is a no-good leech that doesn't care about her in the same way.

Tammy's personality is big on loyalty and honesty; however, her past traumas force her to create unhealthy relationships with the people she is closest to. Still, her natural nature of loyalty keeps her stuck in places she doesn't need to be. Thanks to the amount of dysfunction in her past, it's the place she subconsciously finds the most peace in. That's why it's like drama can't escape her life. For example, her relationship with my brother is unhealthy. I've been telling her that for years. She won't hear me out, though. Now, she really won't listen. She's experiencing PTSD from murdering those two boys, so it's almost impossible to get her to trust anyone when she struggles to trust herself.

The reason why you and Tammy seemed to be so perfect is because inside of her is a broken little girl that is still hurt from daddy issues and the broken relationship she has with her mom. Because of your past failures, you want to be a Mr. Fix It for those you care about. What most people see as strength, you recognized was nothing more than her defense mechanism. You saw that little girl who wanted love, and unlike the rejection she is used to, your loyalty to her made her feel safe. You taught her that vulnerability is a superpower and not a weakness. You allowed her to feel like she could come to you with anything without fear of consequence. It was the first dynamic, outside of her grandmother, that she's had in her life where she didn't feel the need to be a 'people pleaser' to feel secure in her position in your world. The relationship you two started opened the door for her to realize her flaws. It started the discussion of what she really wanted out of life. It was through your loyalty and honesty that she felt safe enough to admit she wanted children and marriage. Before you, she didn't think those things were possible for someone with as much trauma as she's experienced."

"Damn. You're good."

"I know," she responded as she poured another shot for herself. "But I wish I was wrong about Tammy. I honestly love that girl. She's been more of a sibling to me than my own brother, and I hate that I feel like I don't know her anymore.

She's hurting, and before she gets a chance to heal from one thing, life slaps something else on her. Shortly after her father died, we had a session. It was then that she started to open up about the anger she had of him not being present in the first part of her life. She shared how dysfunctional her relationship was with her mother and how she felt rejected by him when she needed him the most. I learned how hard her adolescent years were after being molested as a child by a family member. It didn't help that she didn't have a safe space to open up to because her mother was incapable of providing her what she needed emotionally. Going through that is enough to get a child to question their self-worth or be willing to do anything to get love and approval. Tammy isn't a killer or a drug lord. She did all of those things because she was desperate to do anything to keep the relationships she valued the most.

After those boys were murdered, she shut down on me. The most I've been able to get out of her was just the stuff she would share about you and how it was making her feel at that time. Right now, she's in a space where she doesn't trust a soul around her. She feels like she can't even trust her own thoughts or judgment. Now, she second-guesses everything. The defense mechanisms she's lived with for most of her life are no longer able to protect her anymore. She now sees them for the fallacies they've always been.

I miss my sister, man. I know she's done some fucked up things, and you can do whatever you want to do with all of this information, but she really feels something for you. Professionally, I believe that she keeps hope alive that there is still good in her. I think that's why she's never caused any serious harm your way. Believe it or not, she has a really soft spot in her heart for your siblings, but I'll let her explain all of that to you herself."

"Yo," K.Y. spoke up when she paused for a second to take her shot. "This is a lot of shit to digest. I'm in a place where I don't know what to trust or who to believe. I feel conflicted because a part of me still really cares for her, but I find it really hard to even be nice to her because I feel like she fucked me over. How the hell can I still have feelings for someone who was planning such evil things for my family?"

"I've been doing what I do for years, but I'll be honest with you, I wouldn't want to be in your shoes right now. You're justified to hate Tammy for every evil thing she planned on you and your family. However, you are justified to still have love for her since it was never acted on. I understand the need to have answers for every problem that is presented in life; however, this is one of those moments that really prove to us the things that we believe. From what Tammy has shared with me, you have some sort of belief in God, right?"

He nodded his head.

"Then, the only thing you have to do is believe His word. You have to trust that at this moment, even when you don't know what's best for you, He does. You have to have faith that even when people won't do you right, He will. You have to have hope that even when evil is sitting right at your door that He'll be there to protect you. What do you believe in more right now, him or Him?"

"Are you a doctor or a pastor," K.Y chuckled as he grabbed the bottle to pour himself another shot.

"Listen, I leave the preaching for the pastors. I'm just sharing with you the things that used to give Tammy hope. She believed the things her grandmother preached until she wasn't around to preach it anymore. Now, she doesn't know what to believe, and it's leaving her very susceptible to more trauma. I don't know what to say to take away her pain, and she won't listen to me anyway because she thinks I'm just listening to give my brother information on her. Anyway, that's so far from the truth because I been told her to leave my brother alone."

"For real?"

"Yeah! My brother can't give that girl what she needs. At least, not the man he is now. Sure, if he was willing to have treatment and deal with his own issues, I'm sure he could be that man for her. I just don't think he is ready to put in the amount of work that would be needed for all of that. I wanted him to leave her alone. You know, give her time to heal. They just don't realize how unhealthy their relationship is because it's not as openly toxic as some other people's problems. They don't want to hear me that even drinking a drop of poison is dangerous – and they are two damaged people that won't do the work they need to heal, so they're poisonous for each other.

I'm really sorry you got caught up in all of this foolishness. I know she is too, but I'm not sure if you'll get that from her right now. I don't know what you're walking into with her right now," she said as she slid him a small sheet of paper with an address. "If I had my way, I wouldn't be giving this to you right now. I don't think she's in the right state of mind to handle all of this, but she's adamant that she needs to see you.

I realize that you don't owe me anything, but if your love for Tammy was ever real, please do right by that."

***

"So, did you get the address," Isabella asked as soon as he took got into the car.

"Yeah."

"Well… let me have it," she demanded.

"Didn't I say you were going to have to earn it if I gave it to you?"

All of the alcohol he had been drinking had finally caught up to him and it was obvious by the slur of his words.

"You got any more of that tape and shit at the hotel?"

CHAPTER NINE

He wasn't sure if it was the large amount of alcohol he drank, the fact that he couldn't stop reliving the sweet memories in his head, or the fact that over a year later his heart still refused to mend, but he was determined to get his revenge that night.

K.Y had dreamt about this moment every night for over 365 days. He was ready to make it a reality.

With the help of Josie, K.Y was finally successful in finding out Tammy and Patrick's whereabouts. At first, he thought about just leaving it alone, but after talking to Isabella at the hotel he decided that he needed to move now.

"You don't know how long they're going to be where they're at. If Tammy is vulnerable right now, this is the best time to get her," Isabella suggested as she rode him tirelessly. "Maybe she didn't mean to do you wrong, but the fact is that she did. Now, it's your turn to get what is owed to you."

"I hear you," he responded in between moans. "But how would doing this make me any better than her?"

"Who said anything about being better than her," she responded as she began to bounce on him vigorously. "Stop letting bitches think they can fuck with you. If word got out that you let some broad treat you like this, everyone and their mama would think that they can try you like this.

Let's finish her daddy."

***

"That bitch thought she was about to just play me and live like

51

shit is sweet," he thought as he stuffed his blue backpack with an array of guns and ammo.

"That motherfucker really thought he could fuck the woman I loved and live good off of my hard earned money," he huffed as he became angrier as the sight flashed through his mind of Patrick Bennett enjoying the life that K.Y. had worked so hard to have with Tamia Santiago, the only woman he had ever given his heart to. "Fuck that."

He threw the backpack in the trunk of the rental, plugged the address in the GPS, and threw on some music as he sped off in search of his destination.

After driving close to an hour, he finally pulled up in front of a place he knew all too well. It caused his heart to fall further into his stomach than it had ever been when his nightmare had been confirmed. Tammy had brought Patrick to the exact same bungalow that she had brought him to. The same place where she had opened up and exposed her softer, more vulnerable side to him for the first time, she was now here doing it with another man.

K.Y. thought back to how on that short vacation they had taken together, she had allowed him to feel like a king. She cooked for him and catered to his every need without him even having to ask. He had been sore and achy from the brutal beating he had received in front of Jason's studio in Orlando, FL, and she insisted that they get away so that he could relax.

The pain he had felt that day didn't even come close to the torture he was feeling at that exact moment.

Confusion set in at that moment. A part of him desperately wanted to believe Josie, but after talking with Isabella, he didn't know what to think. His mind kept trying to convince him that she was probably the one who arranged the merciless beating he had received and only catered to his needs in an effort to salvage her guilt.

He made sure to be as quiet as possible as he retrieved the bag he had out of the trunk. He followed the trail that went to the bungalow's entrance.

He stood behind one of the large bushes that was closest to the door, and he used the large window a few feet away to his full advantage.

He watched on in agony as he observed Tammy sashaying from the kitchen to the dining room in the Victoria Secret lingerie he had purchased for her as a gift when they had moved into their condo. *Damn*, he thought to himself as he scanned every inch of her toned and curvy body.

He watched Patrick stare at the feast sitting in front of him. Through the cracked window, the sweet smell of Tammy's home cooking swayed through his nose and reminded him of yet another thing he missed about her. That woman could throw down in the kitchen.

Tammy briefly said grace over the meal and they both sat down to enjoy the feast she had prepared.

K.Y. tried to look away from the seemingly happy couple as they ate, talked, and laughed, but even after the hurt, anguish, and pain she had caused him, everything about Tammy was beautiful, breath taking, and hypnotizing.

After what felt like forever, Tammy got up from the table and cleared away all of the dishes. He watched as Patrick pulled a blunt off of the kitchen table and opened the door that led to the outside patio.

Once Tammy was done cleaning up, she went into the room and resided there for a few moments. K.Y. knew that this was going to be his only opportunity to catch Patrick alone and slipping. Without haste, he moved to finish out his plan.

He slid a gun out of his bag and threw the backpack back on and quietly made his way to where Patrick was.

He was able to use the loud sounds of the ocean to his advantage since Patrick never noticed him as he moved with much determination to finally receive revenge on his enemy.

The night was dark and K.Y. relied on the lights from the stars and the moon above as he finally stood in the presence of the man he had grown to hate with a large passion.

He snuck up behind him, placed the gun to his temple and placed a bullet in the head.

Patrick's demeanor never changed despite the cold steel that was unsuspectingly placed to the soft part of his skull. He continued to casually smoke his blunt.

"Nice to finally meet you motherfucker," K.Y. said through clenched teeth as he tried to remain quiet so he didn't alarm Tammy. "You really thought you were going to break into my home, fuck my girl, take my shit and live happily ever after," K.Y. asked him angrily.

K.Y. was thrown off guard by Patrick's nonchalant demeanor.

Instead of begging for his life, like K.Y had hoped for, Patrick fell into a fit of an evil laughter.

"Pull the trigger then motherfucker. You can't kill what's already dead and I been gone," Patrick said as he exhaled the smoke his lungs had been holding in.

"Anyway nigga, I know my queen taught you that you can't trip on what was never yours to begin with," he stated as his laughter roared again.

K.Y. didn't know what to do next. He didn't come with any other plan since Tammy had told him before that over planning something is the quickest way to ruin one.

He had envisioned killing Patrick many times before, but he wanted to see him squirm first. He wanted to inflict him with as much pain as he had a hand in causing.

"Kyle Cole," Tammy shrieked from behind him as she switched on the patio light. "What the fuck are you doing?"

K.Y. didn't immediately turn around because he wasn't ready to face her yet. He could tell from the cracks in her voice that he had caused her a great deal of pain already. He wanted his revenge, but he wanted her more.

He slowly turned his head and saw something he had never imagined in all of his time dreaming of this moment. He stared down the barrel of what he knew was a loaded gun being held by a dangerous woman.

"Put the gun down, Kyle," Tammy demanded calmly. "You don't want to do this."

"Don't tell me what to do," he responded as he pressed the gun into Patrick's head even more. "You both wasted years of my life and played me and my family. Ya'll owe me, and I'm not doing anything until I get what I deserve."

"I'm not going to keep going back and forth with you. If you don't want to listen, I can just shoot your brains out. Are you going to let that alcohol force you to do something that you'll regret? Because, in case you forgot, I'm the only human alive that knows how to find your siblings. What's it going to be?"

As much as he wanted to empty his clip into Patrick's head, he knew it wasn't a good idea.

"K.Y, please," Tammy pleaded. "If I wanted to harm you or your family, I would have done it already. Put the gun down, and we can talk about whatever you want to know."

She lowered her gun to assure him that she wasn't a threat.

"Listen to the lady. We all know you like to take orders from bitches anyway – thirsty ass nigga. Make sure when you lower that gun that you don't take it off of me until you get to your car because if I get the chance, I'm going to do what Tee originally planned to do to you and your dusty ass mama."

"Rick! What the fuck," Tammy yelled out.

"Nah. This nigga needs to be more appreciative of the fact that he's allowed to breathe right now. How dare he come up on my shit like this?

You think your mom is going to kill her dad, and then you would be the one to off me? You really fucking thought that your family was allowed to just walk around killing off people that Tee cares about?"

Kyle had never considered that fact. If his mom did kill her dad, he didn't want his family to be the cause of anymore of her pain. Regardless of whatever happened, his feelings for her had been genuine, so he was struggling to just turn them off.

"Shut up nigga," Kyle responded as he pushed the gun harder into his skull. He needed a moment to figure out his next move.

"Nah, yo! If you're about that action, then fucking do it. Pull the trigger bitch."

Kyle just wanted a moment of silence to find a peaceful way to end this dangerous conversation. Still, Patrick was beginning to get louder and moved around in his seat like he wasn't fazed by the cold steel on his temple.

"You know they say your mom shot Delino out of fear? I guess the scary bitch raised scary-ass kids too. Well, except for that nigga Keenan, he's the only one out of all of ya'll that seems to have a little heart in him," Patrick fell into another fit of laughter.

Kyle became enraged as he listed to Patrick talk about his family.

"You want to see heart motherfucker?"

"Yeah, bitch. Pull the trigger if you're bad. All of this time, you've been pretending to be a street nigga, so let's see it."

"Please," Tammy pleaded as she realized that Kyle was beginning to crack.

"Fuck that," Patrick screamed loudly. "Pull the fucking trigger bitch cause one of us is dying tonight."

Kyle closed his eyes as he prepared to do it. In that moment,

Tammy rushed to push Patrick out of the way, but in the middle of all of the commotion – the gun went off.

CHAPTER TEN

"In the church, we have grown accustomed to using the word, 'unforgiveness,' but if you've ever tried to type that word into your phone or look up the definition, you would find that that word does not exist."

The church was crowded, and the patrons were intensely listening to the knowledge their pastor preached.

"I know the bible teaches us to 'call those things which are not as though they were', but let's call unforgiveness what it really is: bitterness. When we simply say we are dealing with unforgiveness, we treat it like a disease we are forced to carry instead of realizing that it is a choice that we made once and continue to choose to do every day. We allowed an offense to take root in our hearts, and instead of cutting it out, we would rather let those thoughts grow like weeds.

Why do we expect God to plant great things in hearts that are filled with weeds? What kind of harvest could we truly be expecting?

The bible says, 'Let all bitterness and wrath and anger and clamor and slander be put away from you, along with all malice. Be kind to one another, tender-hearted, forgiving each other, just as God in Christ also has forgiven you.'

Knowing that we were commanded to love and forgive others several times, why do we continue to give permission for bitterness to grow in our hearts? Let me help make everything clear: love is the energy that allows us to produce faith. In turn, our faith knows that we do not have to carry those offenses any longer. When we allow love to create the faith we need for healing and an ability to surrender, we allow God's will to have room to fully operate in our lives. Church, please hear me and hear me good. God cannot do what He wants to do with you as long as you're walking around here bitter.

You may be lying to yourself right now and saying that you operate out of love, but before I close this out, I want to seriously challenge how you view love. We all know 1 Corinthians 13 explains what love is. We've heard that it is patient and kind. We've heard that it isn't easily aggravated and never gives up. I've lost count of how many times I've been told that it keeps no record of wrongdoing, but how many of us can say that we can look at that entire definition of love and say that we apply that to ourselves? Because if we were honest, our thought life is rude. The way we condemn ourselves proves that we aren't willing to suffer long or keep a clean record. Man, the way we quit the moment things get too tough shows that we aren't willing to endure every circumstance on our own. So how can we expect from others what we aren't willing to give to ourselves?"

***

How much did you pay him for his performance?" K.Y asked as he walked into the pastor's office and stood in front of the large oak desk. "Matter of fact, was everyone in the audience acting also? Am I just the only one not aware of what's going on here?"

"I'm not paying anybody to be here," Tammy responded flatly.

"Yeah? Well, I find that very hard to believe since you've spent the last few years putting on one hell of an act for me," K.Y spat back.

"This is why I wanted to meet you here. I knew you were going to be upset, and all I want is the chance to apologize and answer any questions that you have."

"You're green as fuck Tammy. You had those bitches feeding me some shit about you changing plans because you suddenly got a conscience after you realized you weren't really a killer. Couldn't your team of writers come up with anything more clever? Look, I'm just here to get the address for where my family is."

Unable to hide the hurt on her face, Tammy spun around in the oversized office chair she had been sitting in. He had only seen her get emotional once, so he knew he had struck a nerve. Suddenly, he remembered that Josie said Tammy wasn't mentally ready for this. As much as his petty side didn't want to, he decided to take it easier on her.

He finally took a seat in one of the other chairs in the office.

"If that whole story is true, I'm sorry. That was harsh, but I just don't know what the fuck to believe anymore," K.Y spoke up to break the silence.

Not bothering to turn back around, she responded. "I know how you feel. It sucks when you don't know what's real or who you can trust. I'm truly sorry that I messed with your reality."

"Yo, maybe my ears are playing tricks on me, but it almost sounded like you just issued an apology. I didn't even know that you knew what that was," he joked.

He heard her chuckle between sobs. They both sat in silence for a few minutes before she composed herself and turned back around.

"You have every reason to hate me and never speak to me again. I really hope that after this conversation, maybe you'll reconsider those feelings.

Deadass, I had a mad long conversation with your mom a few nights ago, and it really changed how I see things. I know that -," Tammy said before he interjected.

"Hold up, you actually saw my mom," K.Y asked as he sat up in his chair?

"Yeah, but just chill. Nothing happened. I wanted to meet with her first because I wasn't sure how I was going to react to her. For years, I dreamed of getting revenge, so I didn't want to lie to you or make you any promises that I wasn't sure I would be able to keep.

It's true. While I was on one of those hiatuses, I did some things I never thought I would have to do, and it really changed me. That's why a part of me wasn't sure that I would be able to go through with it again, but at the same time, I felt I owed that to my dad."

"I feel you on that because I had this crazy-ass dream that I rolled up on you and Patrick while you guys were enjoying a romantic night together, and all I wanted to do was kill his ass," K.Y chuckled.

"Me and Patrick having a romantic evening? Ha! Yeah, that was definitely a dream. That nigga don't know the first thing about romance. You probably heard the story by now, but when he robbed our apartment that night, that was him being romantic. I guess in his mind, he thought that I would see that he was fighting for me, but it just forced me to face some real fears I have about how I'm living my life.

Anyway, we'll get to that full story later. I just want to put everything in perspective for you. Let me get this stuff off of my chest, and then

I'll tell you all about your siblings.

When I first had Beast set up shop down here, it was for me to get close to Skeme. My grandmother, Estrella, was madly in love with his uncle. But because he faked his death to escape the feds, it was almost impossible to locate him without an inside man."

"So that's the reason why you were all flirty with that nigga," K.Y asked.

"Exactly! When I think about it now, it's so funny to me. I became this huge drug lord that was moving with the mafia and crooked politicians, but one of my first major moves was trying to play cupid. I know that shit made you really uncomfortable, but it was never like that with him. I just needed information that only he knew.

Anyway, after getting set up, this kid I used to deal with back in the day found Jason and told him that your mom was the one who murdered my dad during one of their drug deals. When Beast called to tell me that, I had literally just got through robbing this nigga named Brian, so I was on a natural high. I told them that I was going to avenge my father's death, and at that moment, I meant it. I wanted to find the person who did it, and I wanted to destroy their life like they had done mine. My father and I had finally started working on a real relationship when he was taken from me, so I was moving straight out of my emotions. I thought that every move I made as this kingpin was going to feel good. I fell in love with the power and thinking that I was in control of everyone and everything around me, so it only felt right to declare war on someone who was obviously my enemy.

As you know, in this game, you have to keep your word. Otherwise, niggas will think that you're just all talk or going soft, so even when I felt like throwing in the towel – I couldn't. There were too many niggas who knew that your mom had something to do with my father's death that I wasn't able to just let it go.

The reason you were robbed in front of Beast's studio is because it was obvious to everyone around me that I was starting to care about you. I talked about you way more than I should have. I got sloppy with the information I would share with you, and I had stopped talking about finding your mom. I honestly don't know what it was that made me switch feelings. I think it was how you still wanted me, no matter how much I tried pushing you away. If I presented you with a problem, you would offer a solution. You listened to me. You made me feel safe, understood, appreciated, and loved even when I was doing nothing in return for you. That's why when I got word that a price was put on your head, I rushed to get to you. We went on that little vacation because we had to stay away until the streets knew you were off-limits.

Side note, that was almost impossible to explain. Beast and Patrick couldn't understand why I hadn't ordered the hit or just done it myself. I kept giving excuses. At first, I told them that I was just trying to fatten you up for the slaughter. You know, by helping your moves get bigger so I could clean you out later. They bought it for a while, but then Patrick found out that I knew about your siblings and hadn't used it to my advantage. He took that time to offer up $5,000 dead or alive."

"That's it? Niggas were ready to kill me over five bands," K.Y asked in shock.

"Truthfully, there are some people out there that will do it just to say they did it. It's not as expensive as you would think it is to end someone's life.

Going back to my story, though, once they knew that you were around, and I wasn't actively seeking revenge, things just got really weird. Want to know something else that's weird? Your boy, Rashard, he didn't set you up in the beginning. I had to create a diversion, someone you would focus on so you would never suspect me. The person that stole the stash at the restaurant was me. When I went to the bathroom, I ran to move the product over to my car. Obviously, I lied when I told you about the footage from the cameras."

"Damn."

"I know. Again, I'm really sorry. I did some fucked up things, but I'm going to finally be honest about everything.

Someone from my team had offered Rashard money to pretend to be a drug dealer. He took the offer and then used his money to buy into the game. Once he started stepping into my areas, I had to bring in Tanya, or Isabella as you know her, to help me keep an eye on him.

Unfortunately, dumb, and dumber started doing their own thing. That night when I invited you out to dinner, after being gone for months, I asked you to give me more information on her because I didn't know who she was after she went rogue on the original mission. For years, so many people have warned me about keeping her around, but I refused to see it. I really thought she was down for me like I was for her, but I finally know that was never the case.

That night, I was hoping you would tell me something that would give me some hope that we were on the same side, but that never happened. You probably couldn't tell, but I was at the lowest point of my life at that moment.

My grandmother had just been taken from me. I became a murderer. Patrick and I weren't even speaking. I had lost my best friend, and because of all of the secrets I was holding in, I couldn't share anything with the person I wanted to open up to the most.

Keeping it all in from you was hard, but you came through for me at that moment even when you didn't know how desperately I needed you. You proposed again, and I just wanted to enjoy the bliss I felt from feeling like maybe I really could live a different life with you. Everything after that became real for me about us.

When we robbed King, that was real. He had lost sight of the role he was being paid to play, and he was just moving however he wanted to. He started stepping on the toes of some important people, and I couldn't afford to start a war over his stupidity.

Honestly, that was when I started to see Tanya for who she really was. One minute, she was my friend willing to help me get this kid to play a part. Then, she was suddenly his ride or die. Well, that was until I made her an offer she couldn't refuse. Seeing her switch up so fast every time the money got bigger showed me that her only loyalty is to herself and her pockets.

I was hoping that after the robbery went down that you would sleep with her so that maybe she would open up to you about her issues with me. I really didn't want to believe that everyone had been right about her being flat-out envious. I wanted to think that maybe she was upset about one thing that we could talk about and get past. You see, she's wanted every man I've ever been with. She's wanted my position of power. She hated that my father was in my life and her parents barely paid attention to her. She always had some fucking smart remark whenever something good was going on in my life, but because I could always count on her for whatever I needed – I became blind to her hate.

Anyway, even though I wanted you to sleep with her, I was prepared to fuck the shit out of you the night you came home and found me naked. I was ready to really start taking what we had seriously, and I wanted to be intimate with you.

Truthfully, I've been with Rick for so long, I had no idea what it would be like to be with another man. However, with you, you just made me feel so special and desired that I wanted to know you even more deeply. Obviously, my plan was cut short. I know it sounds crazy that I used PTJ to install our security system and cameras, but it was my company. Despite all of our names being on there, it was my shell company because it helped me clean up some of my money. I had no idea that Patrick had paid one of my installers to put up a camera I had no knowledge of. Playing devil's advocate now, I'm sure that it was hard for him to watch me prepare to love on and be with another man. I know he saw the change in me and felt the distance between us, so I think he lowkey got desperate in that moment. No, I don't support his decision to interfere with my life, but I guess I can understand it.

When you live this role, you really think you're in control of everything and everyone around you. When you have the kind of money and power that Patrick and I have, it's so easy to bully people into doing anything. It gives us this sense of entitlement, and it causes us to stop seeing people as humans with feelings and instead pawns in this game we're playing. It's a dangerous place to be. I liked it for a while, you know when I thought I was the one controlling everything. Then, Patrick started treating me like I was one of the pawns of his game, and then I realized how much that feeling fucking sucks. It was the wake-up call that I needed that anyone – even me – can be touched. It doesn't always matter how much you have or who is in your pockets. You have to reap whatever you sow out."

Tammy took a deep breath. "Well, now that I've said everything I came to say, I have to keep up what I promised.

Truthfully, I knew the story of Kenya and Keenan long before you said a word. I had done all of my research on your family, but I had not located them until after that time we spent at the beach. I know you're probably freaking out thinking that I did some grimey ass shit to them, but you'll see when you talk to them that it wasn't like that at all.

The first time I met Kenya, I just fell in love with her energy. She reminded me of a younger version of myself. She was working as a bottle girl in a strip club. Now, before you get all worked up, I know it's hard to hear that your baby sister was doing that. However, you should know that the niggas who had her usually pimp out girls. Luckily for her, she had a brother who would stop at nothing to protect and provide for her. He got arrested for beating up some niggas who tried her, and that's how I was able to finally locate them. You see, one of your mom's friends had taken them in when she saw them roaming the streets looking for ya'll, and when she told your mom the news the next day, your mom begged her to keep them."

"Nah, Tammy. That can't be right," K.Y said, finally speaking up. "There is no way that my mother knew where they were, and she didn't say anything to me."

"You don't have to believe me. I hope that you'll listen to her with an open mind. I know for a long time you've been really upset with her, but it seems like she wants to be more present now.

When I saw her, she looked amazing. She didn't look like someone who had ever been strung out on drugs. Apparently, she's been clean now for over a year. She just wanted to really get on her feet before trying to get you guys together. Anyway, Ms. Rosie was the woman who took in your siblings."

At that moment, he knew she wasn't lying. He always thought it was weird how she managed to vanish overnight.

"Originally, she planned to just love them as if they were her own. Ms. Rosie wanted to get them away from the drug dealing and drug-using, but someone caught her slipping one day. One of her ex-boyfriends had laced her blunt, and before she knew it, she was hooked on the same stuff she wanted to get away from.

The man she was dealing with was heavy in the human trafficking game, and he fell in love with your sister. That was the only reason he wouldn't separate her from Keenan, and that's how she got the chance to work in one of his strip clubs instead of being one of his hookers. Like you said, she is a genius, and even though she didn't have much street smarts, she knew to play on his affection for her.

When I finally found them, I went to the club, and I sat in her section. I spent a lot of time just watching her and how she moved. Understandably, she's really guarded, so I knew I had to come correct when I finally made my move. After talking to her for so long, I started to feel bad that she was out in this huge world without a figure in her life that would protect her. Yeah, she has her brother there as her muscle, but she doesn't have someone to help check her thoughts or how she's feeling emotionally. Unlike me, she didn't have an Estrella Cruz in her corner. She didn't have a mom she could rely on, so I played off of that. That was my angle.

To her, I was like a big sister that she never had, so she would share everything with me. She even started giving me the details of the niggas whole operation, so it made it so easy to crush him when the time came."

"So, if you took him down, then where are they now," K.Y asked as he sat up.

"Sadly, your sister and brother fell in love with the streets.

I tried to convince them to come look for you a couple of times, but they had this idea in their minds that you didn't want them. Apparently, they had heard about the times where you complained about having to be the responsible one for them, so they didn't want to be a burden on you. When I left you for good, I gave them a huge chunk of change, thinking they would come here, but instead, your sister moved her hustle to Atlanta. Shit, I even sent her all of that money you had given me, hoping she would desire a different life."

"Her hustle? What the hell kind of hustle can a young girl like her really have?"

"Her ability to separate a man from his cash is truly in a league of its own," Tammy responded. "As much as I don't want her in this game, there is a part of me that trusts myself when I think about how much she's going to be good."

"I don't even know how to respond to that. I have a million questions going through my mind, and some of them I don't think I'm ready to receive an honest answer for. What the fuck?"

K.Y slouched down in the chair as the weight of his thoughts put him in a state of mind he had never experienced before. He took a deep breath as he tried to imagine having his family back in his life.

"This shit is tough, so I can't imagine what you're feeling right now. I'm going to text you your sister's address," Tammy said as she pulled out her phone. "After you spend some time with your mom, you can go find them, and I'm sure they'll help put your mind at ease.

Neither one of them know the whole truth. Between you and me, I really started to care for your sister, and I just can't bring myself to tell her that I had intentions of using her. She's been through way too much to hear any more bad news, but I can understand if you feel the need to fill them in with everything."

After Tammy was done speaking, they both sat in silence for a few minutes. Neither one of them knew how to proceed next.

"Well," K.Y spoke up. "I guess I should try to go put my family together now."

"Yeah. I know you've been looking forward to this day. When I met your mom, she was at the house, so you should probably be able to find her there."

"Thank you," he responded. "So, what are you going to do now," he asked Tammy.

"I have no idea. I want to leave this shit so bad, but when you're ass-deep in the mud with the mafia – walking away isn't usually an option.

I really need to put some serious thought into my next move."

"Whatever you decide to do, please just be careful. It really sounds like Isabella, or Tanya, whatever her real name is, has a serious plan to take you down for good."

"Ugh," she grunted as she rolled her eyes. "The part of me that still feels like a boss wants to say that I have this under control. I'm prepared to lose a few battles in the process, but that doesn't matter because I plan to win the war in the end. Then, the part of me that is ready to be real with myself reminds me that no one is ever really in control when playing this game."

"Just be careful, please," he pleaded as he stood up.

"I will," she responded as she did the same. She walked from behind the desk to face K.Y.

"I'm afraid to ask, but a hug would be really nice right now," Tammy said as she put her arms out.

Without hesitation, he pulled her in and embraced her tightly.

"I'm sorry about your grandmother Tee. I know losing the backbone to your family is hard as fuck."

Immediately, Tammy started crying. She used that moment to let go of all of the pain she had been hiding, even to herself.

"I don't know if I could ever get over this pain," she mustered in between sobs. It was hard to hear everything she was saying as she muffled everything into his shirt, but by the way she melted into his arms was proof that she was finally getting some weight off of her shoulders.

"Do you know her family wouldn't even let me be a part of her funeral? In their eyes, I was only a 'family friend,' so they didn't want to hear shit I had to say. They sold her home and everything in it, and they cremated her without giving her a decent funeral. Those motherfuckers didn't do shit for her while she was alive. I did everything I could for her while she was here, and now she's gone. Most people give their dogs a better homegoing service than she got."

Tammy started crying uncontrollably, and Kyle just held her while she let it all out.

"Man," she calmly said before she took a deep breath. "I needed to get that shit off of my chest. I just don't have anyone else I feel comfortable talking about this shit with. I missed you. I missed being able to have this."

"Damn," K.Y said as he stepped back from her. "I feel like shit now. I have to tell you something too.

It's so fucked up how all of this played out. You just confessed to something I've wanted to hear forever, and I feel like now everything is messed up.

That night, when I was given the address to meet you here, I also caved and gave the address to Isabella.

She said she had a sure plan to give us the revenge we were both looking for, and I was so drunk. I know that doesn't make things better now, but at the time, I just didn't know what to believe. Your girl was up there trying to tell me that you cared about me, but then Isabella reminded me of how your actions proved otherwise. I just didn't know what to do. I'm sorry."

To his surprise, Tammy pulled him in for a loving kiss. They embraced for a few minutes.

"No need to apologize," Tammy responded as she pulled away. "We wouldn't be in this mess if I didn't come up here fucking with your life. It's like my grandmother kept warning me, if I left the snake playing in the grass for too long – it was bound to find and bite me. Thanks for the heads up, at least." She turned to head for the door.

"Wait, before you leave, I just want to know. What happens next…you know… with us? I know shit is crazy, but how can we just act like we don't have these feelings or like we don't really care for each other," K.Y asked.

She turned and faced him.

"Honestly, I don't know what to do, but I know before I do anything – I have to figure out who I am. This shit has taught me that I'm not a murderer. I hate the guilt that comes from crime, and I'm really not as mean as I feel I have to be to people. Ironically, I spend most of my time acting in this role, but I'm finally at a point where I don't want to play anymore. I want out, and I know I need to do it alone.

For years, I was in this relationship with Patrick, and now that I don't want to live the same life, I don't know what that means. I no longer wish to be the woman I used to be for him, and I know that I'm not ready to be the woman you deserve. I don't know how to be something for someone else that I don't know how to be for myself. As crazy as it all sounds, I think I really need to learn to love and forgive myself before I can give any part of me to anyone else. Even to you – someone I've really grown to love and care for. If I jumped into anything as this woman I am today, I know I'm going to fuck that up. I don't want to do that with you.

I think after everything that I've put you through, you deserve transparency and honesty. I don't know what that looks like as a woman living a legit life.

I *need* time to see if I'm finally over Patrick. I *need* time to mourn my grandmother. I *need* time to fix things with my mom while she's still alive. I *need* to forgive myself for things I've done.

I know that I can ask you to wait, and you'll probably do it, but that won't be fair to either of us because I'm not sure where this next chapter of my life is going to lead me.

Live your life, baby. My grandmother taught me enough that I have confidence to know that what is meant to be mine will always be there for me when I'm ready.

No matter what though, just know that I *really* do love you."

***

Tammy walked out of her cousin's church feeling an array of feelings. For once, she finally understood why her grandmother used to always say, "where the Spirit of the Lord is, there is freedom." She wasn't sure if it was the inspiring message that was preached or if it was because she had finally told the truth about everything, but Tammy felt amazing. For the first time since her grandmother had passed, Tammy could almost feel her presence. It was peaceful.

Kyle's hugs and affection were an added bonus. She didn't know how he was going to take seeing her, but she certainly didn't expect him to be so open.

She chose the church as her meeting place for a few reasons. Still, the main one was her desperation to feel anything other than the emotions she had grown accustomed to living with. Losing her grandmother left her with an emptiness she had never felt. Sure, she had experienced death before, but when she lost Estrella, she lost her sanctuary. Her grandmother's house was the one place in the world where nothing else mattered. She could always count on a good meal and life-changing advice. Tammy was free to grow in a space that was free of fear, judgment, and full of love. She missed that more than anything.

She lost herself the day Estrella was murdered. Who was going to keep her in line? Who was going to remind her to take a break or to slow down every now and then? Who was she supposed to be without the relationships that she felt defined her?

To help her out during those nights that felt impossible to survive, Tammy started reading the journals that her grandmother had written while she was alive. They were full of some of her favorite sayings, but it also exposed how much she allowed the poetry that was in her bible to change everything about her. It was filled with scriptures and prayers. It didn't matter what she was dealing with, Estrella always found comfort in the word of God, and Tammy was willing to see if it could somehow help her now.

Before she walked out, she paused to take a moment to fully enjoy everything she was feeling because she knew everything was about to change.

Tammy wasn't even halfway down the church steps before problems came looking for her.

"Tamia Santiago, do you have any idea how long I've been waiting for this moment?"

"Detective Harris, how nice of you to interrupt my peaceful Sunday morning. How can I help you," Tammy responded.

"You can't, but I can help you if you'll finally start talking. You see, for all these years, you've only ever been untouchable because no one was willing to talk. Well, now I have a witness who has proof and is willing to testify."

Tammy didn't lose the bounce in her step as she continued in the direction of her car. Detective Harris had been a thorn in her side from the moment she stepped foot in Orlando, Florida, as a drug kingpin.

"If you had enough to get me, you would have done it already. Now, if you'll excuse me, I would really appreciate it if you left me the fuck alone."

"Not this time, Ms. Santiago."

As soon as she turned the corner, she saw the other officers in suits. She already knew what that meant.

"Tamia Santiago, you are under arrest."

CHAPTER ELEVEN

Isabella had been impatiently waiting in her bedroom for hours. She was finally about to celebrate all of her dreams coming true. Tammy was about to be put away. So that left her an open opportunity for the man that should have been hers all along.

"Finally," she said as she jumped up to answer the knocks coming from her front door. She took a moment to admire herself in the mirror before opening it. She didn't want to waste any time, so she was only in her hot pink lingerie.

"Yo," Patrick said as he walked past her without so much as a glance. "Why the fuck is you naked?"

"What's the problem? Don't I have a nice body to look at?" Isabella did a little twirl to give him access to see everything.

"It's aight. Anyway," Patrick said as he took a seat on her couch. "Why the fuck did you call me over here?"

"Well, I know that you're probably upset that Tammy did you the way that she did, so I wanted to be the first to tell you that she finally got what was coming to her."

"Why would you think that I wanted revenge from a woman I was with for mad years?"

"Why wouldn't you should be the real question!" She sashayed over to join him on the couch. Again, he didn't seem interested in the show she was trying to put on for him.

"For years, you held Tammy down. How the fuck is she going to repay you by lying to you for all of this time while she fell in love with some bum-ass corner boy? How the fuck can she just make you look like a fool out here? I know you aren't going to stand for that, and that's why I did something about it. As we speak, her ass is being taken to jail."

"What," he exclaimed as he sat up in his seat. "What the fuck do you mean she's on her way to jail, and how do you know what's going on?"

"Well, I figured I would take care of both of your problems at one time, so I set that nigga's house on fire with his mom in it. With me, another eyewitness, and her fingerprints all over the stuff that was used to set the house on fire, there is no way she'll see life as a free woman. I made it way too easy for Detective Harris to put her away once and for all. He has my statement, proof that her phone bounced off of one of the towers around the time of the fire, and he has her fingerprints on the evidence. She's done."

Instead of being all over her like she had expected, Patrick fell into a fit of laughter.

"I've been telling Tee for years that you were a fucking snake, but I honestly didn't think that you were this crazy, or I would have handled you myself a long time ago."

Without any warning, Patrick turned to face Isabella and put his large hands around her neck.

"I know Tammy said you were freaky," she struggled to say. "But it's hard to breathe."

She started swatting his hands, hoping that this was his idea of foreplay. But as she struggled to get any oxygen, she quickly realized that she wasn't going to get the happy ending she had hoped for.

Patrick usually didn't get his hands dirty, but there wasn't a thing in the world he wasn't willing to do for Tammy.

"Bitch, the only reason you've had close access to anyone during this time is because we thought it was better to play you close as Tammy's plan to get you out of the grass was in motion. I just want you to know that you weren't slick. You've been running around with my sister this entire time so that we always had eyes and ears on you while you were free – not because we liked your ass. We'll find some way to beat this case, but your ass won't get the satisfaction of enjoying any of her pain, you dusty, broke, crazy, lazy, bitch."

Patrick squeezed tighter as his anger just continued to climb. All he could think about at that moment was what Tammy could be going through. Despite her living the life of a drug lord, he knew she wasn't built for jail. Then, the realization hit him. He couldn't come to her rescue like he genuinely wanted to because he had committed to giving her the space she asked for. After his interference and refusal to provide her with the love she was searching for, she asked him to respect her need to try to move on without him. Sure, she would be happy that he helped her out, but he didn't want to do anything that could jeopardize his chances of getting her back. He knew he couldn't love her the way Kyle did, but he was willing to learn to try. Tammy had just requested too much too fast, and he didn't know how to be what she needed at that moment. For years, he thought she was happy with the way their relationship was. Before meeting Kyle, she had never brought up marriage, so he was surprised to see her so delighted at the idea of being a wife. He saw her blossom into a softer side of herself, and he struggled to adapt to this new woman. He figured that maybe if he ignored it that it would just stop, but instead, it drove a wedge between the woman he loved so much.

Patrick was inundated with his emotions and thoughts, and that was why he instinctually grabbed Isabella to shut her up. But he just realized that he would never find out who the other eyewitness was if she died. He let her go so that she could have a moment to catch her breath and give him the information he needed, but the way her body thudded down to the floor immediately let him know he was too late.

COMING SOON
CHARGE IT TO THE GAME 4

"Let's go, Santiago," the guard yelled as he unlocked her cell door. "It's time to get you in population."

"Population," she asked as she stood to her feet. "There has to be some kind of mistake. I'm not even supposed to be here. I didn't do anything. I haven't talked to my lawyer, and Detective Harris still hasn't talked to me since arresting me. What the hell is going on?"

"Listen, princess," the guard responded. "I know you're used to calling all of the shots out in the streets, but in here, you do what I tell you to do. All of that other shit isn't any of my business. My job is to get you in an orange jumpsuit and out of these holding cells. Now, let's go."

Tammy was furious. In that moment, all she wanted to do was scream, cry, and hit the guard in his face, but she knew that it would just make everything worse. She felt her anxiety climbing and figured that it would be in her best interest to follow him because she wasn't going to talk herself out of this one.

If one of those bitches try me, she thought as she followed him down the poorly lit hallway. *I'm going to destroy them. No,* another thought interjected. *That would just add on to whatever Detective Harris is holding me for. I don't want to get any more time than he's trying to give me now. I can't mess this up. I can't let my emotions get the best of me. I can't do time in jail – I'm not built for this. I can't freak out now. I just can't fall apart. God, please help me keep it all together.*

Luckily for Tammy, they reached their destination before she had a chance to fall any deeper in thought than she had already been.

"Here," he said as he passed her two sets of orange jump suits, a pair of slides, and a bag with her pillow and bed linen. "In the bag, you'll also find a bar of soap, a toothbrush, and toothpaste. On Wednesdays, we give you an hour in the library. It was that little room we passed just before getting in here. On Sundays, you can go to church in the morning if you want. You just have to make sure to sign up for it. If you need anything else, like lotion, socks, or underwear, you're going to have to pay for it out of your commissary money.

Once you're done changing, I'll take you to go meet your new roommates."

Tammy turned to go change in the small bathroom. Even though she wasn't going to avoid going to population, she took her time to for every step. She wanted to enjoy the last minute of peace and solitude she had remaining. Tammy was afraid of the uncertainty of what was coming next. Were the girls going to be cool and funny like they were on Orange is the New Black, or were they in search of their new top dog like in Wentworth? For the first time in her life, Tammy was finally ready to go in search of the woman she really was and not the person everyone thought she should be, so it was depressing to know that she would have to play another part just to survive.

Who is the jail house version of Tamia Santiago? Is she a bitch? Does she fight and curse a lot more than usual? Is she peaceful and calm like the Muslim niggas in all of the urban fiction books? God, please help me, she prayed out again.

In that moment, Tammy realized that she had prayed more since having those cold cuffs slapped on her wrist than she's ever done in her life. *Is this a part of the Tammy I have to be in jail? Does she pray a lot and rely on God more?*

"Let's go Santiago," the guard called out. "I got other shit to do today."

Although she was already dressed, she couldn't bring herself to open the door. She wasn't ready to find out what jail was really like. She had always imagined that she was too good to get caught slipping. Honestly, she never considered that she would ever end up in jail. Sure, she always preached about it when trying to get other people around her to do right, but she just never thought she would be here.

"Give me one minute," she cried out as she tried to buy herself more time. "I'm almost done," she lied.

"No, you're not," he screamed back. "I can hear you pacing around in those cheap ass jail slides, so I know you're already dressed. Get out here."

Damn. How the fuck am I going to survive in here playing any kind of part if this nigga can catch me slipping so early? God, I know I don't really fuck with you like that. Wait, can I curse when I pray? I mean, I feel like the bible says to come as I am, and I curse, so that's cool, right? Anyway, I need you to help me through this. I know I've said in the past that I would change if you helped me out, but I really mean it this time. If you'll get me through this, then I'm going to do something different with my life. I can't make any promises like I would preach like my cousin, but I will try to be a better human. Please just help me through this.

"Ok," she called back to him. "But can we please stop by the library first? I know it's not Wednesday, but I've never had to do this before, and I think having the chance to read a book will really help me out. I know you technically don't have to do anything but your job, but I would really appreciate it," she pleaded.

"If you get your ass out of there in the next ten seconds, I'll take you."

Tammy took a deep breath and quickly grabbed her things.

"Who knew that a trip to the library could make a woman move so fast," he chuckled.

For the first time since being arrested, Tammy let out a soft laugh herself.

"I just really like books. I wish I would have listened to my grandmother and focused more on my poetry and writing than I did doing other shit. I know if anything is going to help me out, getting the chance to read a good book will help."

She followed the guard as he walked her back through the hallway to the small library. When he opened the door, she was disgusted to see the way the books were treated. There was no organization to what was there, and from what she could tell, there weren't a lot of selections that she really wanted to read.

"I see mad bibles and ripped up magazines, but where are the good urban fiction novels or some poetry or something," she asked as she skimmed through the books that were there.

"Look, the warden is really picky about what kind of books are allowed in here. Anyway, you just said you need to be more focused on your writing and shit, right? Why not take the time to do that? Here," he said as he passed her a stack with a few sheets of blank paper and three small pencils that didn't have erasers. "I know it's not a lot, but it's a couple of the items we give you guys in here. That should be enough to at least get you started."

"You know," she said as she took the stuff he was giving her and placed them in her mesh bag. "Ya'll guards aren't as bad as they make ya'll seem on TV. You seem pretty cool. What's your name anyway."

"C.O Mack and not everyone is relaxed. I'm just doing this while I finish school, so I do what is asked of me while trying to treat you guys like I would want someone treating me. Don't get it twisted, though. There are a lot of people in here looking for that next promotion, so they do everything by the fucking book."

Tammy had a million questions she wanted to ask, but she was terrified that he might know who she was or someone who was connected to her team. How would niggas on the outside want to work with her if they knew that jail time was so scary to her?

"Luckily for you, niggas is pretty chill in this unit. There is one chick, though, that they say is crazy. Apparently, she swallowed a battery so they could send her to psych. I guess her plan was to try to escape when she was in there since they aren't handcuffed, but it obviously didn't work out. Now, she just spends most of her time sleeping. The other girls you'll be locked down with just keep getting small time for petty shit. They don't start a lot of trouble cause they are just trying to get back out to their drugs. C.O Robinson is a bitch, so make sure you follow her instructions. Other than that, just try to lay low and write. Oh, make sure you write your books in the third person or something. You don't want anyone in here thinking you got a diary with confessions. Otherwise, those niggas will shake down your cell every damn day."

Shake down, she thought. *What the fuck is that? I thought that shit was just for T.V.* Tammy wanted to ask him, but she was so grateful that he started pouring out some of the information she needed. It offered her more relief to know what she was going to be facing when she got in there.

"Bet," she responded. "I really appreciate all of your hospitality C.O Mack, so I think I'm finally ready to go."

Even though the library wasn't very far from population, the journey felt treacherous to her. The sound of their footsteps echoed eerily off of the drab off-white walls while her mind kept rehearsing every possible worst-case scenario in her head.

"Ladies", C.O Mack called out as they approached population. "Your new roommate is here, so make sure you play nice."

He unlocked the large door, and Tammy followed him inside. Tammy wasn't sure what she had expected, but this definitely wasn't it. The room had two separate parts. On one side, there was a large table, one window, some chairs, and a television. The other room had four desks and two bunk beds that were all bolted to the ground.

"Hey! My name is Tina Brown," the youngest, most pale girl spoke as she jumped up. "Let me help you put on your bed linen. That fitted sheet is always the trickiest."

Tammy paused for a moment because she wasn't sure how to respond. On one hand, she appreciated the offer, but she had read enough urban fiction books to know that no one is ever really your friend in jail.

"First time," she asked when she noticed Tammy's hesitancy.

"Yeah," Tammy responded as she scanned the room for everyone's responses. She noticed the open bed that was probably hers. It was the one that was above a young woman sleeping soundly while everyone else watched.

"The first time is the hardest – especially if you don't know when you're getting out or what to expect in this process. I'm Christina Brown, by the way. I've been in and out of this place since I turned eighteen a few years ago."

Christina was a tiny thing. If she hadn't revealed that she was in her early twenties, Tammy would have assumed that she was too young to be locked up with grown women. She was only five feet tall and couldn't be any more than a hundred pounds. Her baby blue eyes were impossible to miss. Although she obviously needed dental work, her smile was so inviting. There was something about her that seemed genuine. Sadly, Tammy wasn't sure if she was able to trust that feeling because she had also felt the same way about meeting her old best friend, Tanya Isabella.

"Come on," she said as she took Tammy's bag to find the fitted sheet. "Lunch will be here soon, so let's get you settled. We usually go on lockdown after lunch, so you'll want to have it ready."

Because of some of the shows that Tammy had seen, a part of her felt like she couldn't let the other girls think she was soft. She had just allowed the smallest girl in the room to take her stuff from her after all. Again, she scanned the room to see everyone else's response. To her surprise, one of the other girls went back to reading her book. The other one got up, grabbed her stuff, and headed to the back of the room where the showers were.

Almost as if she had sensed what Tammy was thinking, Tina spoke up. "Being locked up here isn't as bad as being locked up in other places. Sure, there are some jails out there that I would have never tried to grab your stuff from you, but it's cool in here. A lot of the girls that end up in here don't have to do a lot of time, or they are on their way to prison, so it's not a lot of drama usually.

Anyway, can you share some stuff about you? What's your name? Why are you in here?"

"My name is Tammy, and I'm honestly not sure why I'm here. I was arrested and booked, but I never got the chance to get any information as to why I'm in here."

"They do that sometimes. That's their way of getting you to sweat it out. I wouldn't be surprised if they make you wait a few days before coming in here to have that conversation with you. This is their way to get you to think of every bad thing you've ever done in your life, so they can hopefully get a confession out of you. I don't like being in here, so I just hear whatever they tell me and then sign my little deal so I can go about my business."

"You know that's part of how they keep you in this system, right? Usually, a deal comes with probation or something, and their goal isn't for you to ever be off of that. They want you to end up right back in here," Tammy responded.

"Oh, you're one of those conspiracy theorists. You'll love Manda when she wakes up. She's always saying similar shit, but I just hate being in here. I wish I didn't do the things that land me here, but I can't help it. I like drugs, drinking, and partying, but it's always the reason I end up back in here. This time it was because I stole some shit to get some money. I wanted to get high, and money has been tight since my baby daddy won custody of the kids. After that, I just started partying harder cause when I'm high, I don't feel anything but happy. When I'm in here, I'm forced to think about shit soberly, and it sucks.

Anyway," she said as she stood up. Judging from how much she struggled to get the sheet on, Tammy was glad that she decided to let her help. "Lunch is about to be coming up soon. During feeding time and when we have rec is the only time you'll see your bottom bunk roomie. Her name is Manda Santana. She's cool, but just don't fuck with her. She dated some drug dealer who got her strung out on heroin. Then, one day he, his money, and his drug supply vanished, so she had to learn the hard way that her habit wasn't easy to keep up with. She had a robbery ring operation going on for a while. They stole all kinds of shit. If you ask her where the money went, she'll tell you that it all went to drugs. Don't ask her about how much time she has, though, because it will just piss her off. The other girls and I think it's around 20 years, but don't trust us because we ain't lawyers," she giggled. "Adrianna is the Mexican girl, but we all just call her Ari," Tina nodded in the direction of the young girl who was reading to herself. "I don't know a lot about her because she doesn't talk about herself very much. She'll join in with us during games or conversations, but that's about it. The dark-skinned girl is Keisha. For some reason, I'm just really afraid of her. But she's never done anything to me or any of the girls in here. I just feel like she would beat me up if I said something crazy because whenever we watch our ratchet reality shows, she always says, 'I'll beat dat bitch ass.' I believe she could really do it."

Just as she had finished her final sentence, Keisha walked out of the showers.

"Bitch, you in here talking about me again," she asked as she put her stuff down on her bed.

This is it, Tammy thought as she tensed up. *This will be my first real experience with jail life.*

"Yeah," she responded boldly. "I was just giving the new girl a little a little information about everyone she was locked up with."

Tammy noticed that Keisha relaxed a little bit as she grabbed her lotion. "Well bitch make sure you tell her that you like to run your fucking mouth too." Tina and Keisha both erupted in laughter.

"Like she said, I do like to run my mouth, but I won't do shit. I'm as scared as they come. At least I won't lie about it like other people. My mouth is crazy, but I'm not. I'll talk my shit, but I'll also stay in my corner."

All of the girls laughed at her honest confession.

"Inmates! It's lunchtime," Tammy heard as the large door swung open.

"This is C.O Robinson," Tina whispered to Tammy. "Do what she tells you – how she tells you to do it, and you can usually avoid a problem. I can't guarantee that it will because she is always searching for issues."

Since the first time Tammy had gotten to population, she saw Manda's face. She was beautiful and had rich chocolate skin. Judging from her hair texture, Tammy wanted to assume she was also an Afro Latina. Still, she knew better than to just assume.

"Listen," Manda said as she took her seat for lunch. "If any of ya'll don't want your food, I'll eat it."

"We know," Tina said as she sat across from her. "You say that at every meal because all you do is eat, shit, and sleep."

"So, we have fresh meat," C.O Robinson said as she handed Tammy her lunch.

She wasn't sure how to respond to her since she had heard so many rough things about her, so she chose to stay silent and just join the other girls.

"I'm guessing your mama never taught you anything about manners," she said as she began pouring their mandated eight ounces of milk. "Since you can't say thank you, I guess you don't need this either."

The part of Tammy that inherited her dad's dynasty wanted to fight for it, but a huge part of her didn't feel like it was worth it. At that moment, Tammy decided that this new role she was willing to play would choose peace over everything else. Instead of lashing out, like she would have in the past, Tammy chose to be silent.

At that moment, she thought of her grandmother, Estrella Cruz, and she found herself getting emotional.

Before eating, Tammy bowed her head and began to pray. *Fuck! Not now. I can't do this here, and I certainly can't do it in this exact moment. Everyone will think I'm soft as fuck, and this bitch will think she broke me down. Lord, if you will just get me through this moment, I promise I'll learn to be silent more.*

She knew she hadn't been praying very long, but Tammy was relieved to see that C.O. Robinson was gone.

"That's fucked up that she really didn't give you any milk," Manda said before she shoved her last spoonful of food in her mouth.

Nah. It's fucked up that they actually serve us this shit. Tammy used her spoon to move her mushy meal around her plate.

"If you don't eat now," Tina spoke up. "It will be hours before you get to eat again. The next meal isn't any better than this one. It will be two bologna and cheese sandwiches, a bag of chips, a banana, and a cup of milk. Well, that is if you don't manage to get under Robinson's skin again."

"I've been in this hell hole for a long ass time, and I've never seen her act that way with anyone before. Ya'll know each other on the outside or something," Manda asked.

"How can you ever see anything when you're always sleeping," Tina joked.

"Bitch, now is not the fucking time to pop off with your shit unless you want to get slapped too," Manda retorted.

Tina didn't respond. Instead, she used that as a moment to jug down her milk.

"Seriously yo, do you know her?"

"No, I don't," Tammy responded earnestly.

"You might not know her, but everyone knows who the fuck you are. That shy shit isn't going to work in here, and it's humorous that you want to act so holy." For the first time since Tammy arrived, Arianna spoke up.

Uh-oh.

"Clearly, you have an issue with me, so let's address it. What's up," Tammy asked.

"You killed my fucking brother, bitch!"

Tammy immediately saw the faces of the two young men she had murdered in her mind. She scanned her face expeditiously, searching for any trace that she might have been related to either of them. A part of Tammy knew that this could have been a trap, but a larger part of her was tired of carrying that secret for so long.

"Bitch, who the fuck is your brother," Keisha asked boldly.

"Francisco Gonzales and he was a great father and brother until he got hooked on the product that she's pumping in these streets. You think just because you have other people doing your dirty work that we didn't know you were the one responsible for so many deaths in our community. I hope they're charging you with every life you've ever fucked up."

Tammy was speechless.

"Now you want to be silent? Any other time, you would be out here calling shots and hiring hits, but now you want to be fucking quiet?"

"Look, Adrianna, I really don't know how to respond to you right now. Yes, I've made a lot of fucked up choices in my life," was all she was able to say before she was cut off.

"So you admit that you killed my brother?"

"I never said that. My terrible choices in life affected a lot of people. I'm genuinely sorry that any choice in my life had a negative impact on yours. I used to be selfish as fuck, so I never stopped to consider anyone else's feelings. I'm sorry for anything I did to you."

The room became jarringly silent.

Without finishing her food, Ari got up and went back to her bunk. Manda immediately grabbed her plate.

Tammy had officially lost her appetite. She got up and went to get her stuff to take a shower.

Is this a safe decision right now? The bitch didn't respond and for all I know she's in here for battery or something. Tammy's mind began to race with all sorts of worst-case scenario situations. She decided not to let her thoughts control her.

The hot water felt refreshing on her skin. Although it was much hotter than she usually would have showered, she just enjoyed the peace that the solitude was providing her. It felt good to not have people blowing down her phone for everything. Even though she was in jail, a part of her felt relief from the pressures of just living her life.

More than anything, Tammy wanted to pull out a sheet of paper and one of those raggedy pencils to finally tell her story. Still, she remembered what C.O. Mack had warned her. The last thing she needed was a written confession to any crime – no matter how beautifully she would have written it.

After her shower, Tammy immediately went to her bed. All of the other ladies were sleeping, and Tammy felt like she could use a nap also.

Before she had a chance to fall into a deep sleep, she was jolted awake.

"Santiago, let's go. You've been summoned," C.O. Mack called out.

She sat up frightened. Luckily for her, none of the other girls were awake to see.

"Who is it," Tammy asked once they left earshot of the other girls.

"You're finally getting the conversation you wanted with Detective Harris."

Shit.

"I hear you've been pissing people off since you've been here. That was quick as fuck."

"Nah," Tammy responded. I literally didn't say a single word to her and she spazzed on me."

"I was just messing with you. She told the rest of us that you guys had some sort of issues outside of these walls."

"That's the thing – I honestly have no idea who she is. What kind of issues could we have?"

"Apparently you guys were sharing the same man."

Tammy laughed.

"That's impossible. The only nigga I rocked with would never rock with her."

"Well, if you let her tell it. You and sis was out here sharing that nigga Rick."

At that moment, it felt like her stomach had fallen and hit the ground. Sure, she said she wanted to move on to find herself without him, but she had loved that man more than anything at one point in her life. Hearing that hurt because in all of the years they had been together, she never once entertained the thought that he might have been unfaithful.

Before she could fully process all of her emotions, they arrived at the small interrogation room.

"You're always fly, but you look so much better in orange," Detective Harris spat as soon as she walked in the room.

"Detective Harris, do you mind explaining to me why the fuck I'm here," Tammy asked

"Don't play dumb with me, Tee. There are a million reasons why you should be in that fucking jumper. I just finally got something that would stick."

"Well, do you mind sharing that with me? It would be really nice to know what the hell is going on."

She was having a hard time maintaining her confidence, but she managed to pull it together like she always did.

"Well, originally, I only planned to charge you for murder and first-degree arson. But you decided to leave me with no choice but to finish you off with the death of your frenemy, Isabella, or Tanya, or whatever the fuck her name is.

The jury is going to love making an example out of you. I can't wait to see their faces when they find out that you and a group of your employees set fire to a home. You knowingly planned the murder of Sasha Cole since you were upset about her killing your father. Once you found out that your best friend had turned and was acting as our intel, you had her murdered."

Tammy was numb. She promised Kyle that she wouldn't seek revenge. If she really was dead, would he ever believe she had nothing to do with it? Although Tanya Isabella had been a terrible friend to her, she just couldn't manage to forget all of the good times they had shared together. In her mind, their friendship was real; however, she was finding that the betrayal was starting to hurt worse than the loss of their friendship.

Ask for a lawyer.

"I don't know what you're talking about," Tammy responded emotionless.

"Of course, a real criminal never tells his dirt. You'll take all of your secrets to your grave, but you can bet that I will make you pay for every one that is exposed to me."

Say you want a lawyer.

"Let me guess, you're here to offer me a deal if I tell you what you want to know," she chuckled.

"Nah, love. Those offer days are over. I actually just came to gloat. It seems like every time I'm satisfied with the thought that I'm beating you, the universe just sends me something else to finish you off with."

Again, Tammy's stomach felt like it hit the floor. She was beginning to get nervous. Usually, Detective Harris was always on a mission to get her to talk.

Breathe. Relax. Don't let him see you sweat. Stop engaging with him and lawyer up!

"I really have no idea what you're talking about. I would have never killed Sasha Cole, and the last time I saw Isabella, she was alive and well. I think your obsession with proving yourself is starting to make you desperate." Despite her anxiousness overtaking her, Tammy sat back in her seat and relaxed.

"I've watched every minute of footage we have of you in here, and I haven't figured out how you ordered her hit, but I will figure it out. I can promise you that. I wonder how your baby will feel when he or she only knows you through prison bars."

"Baby," a confused Tammy responded. "Clearly, you have me mistaken for someone else."

Stop believing shit this man says. He's trying to get you to crack. Ask for a fucking lawyer.

"Every inmate is tested for shit when they come up in here. One of them is a pregnancy test. Congratulations, mom. I'm sure your child will have a promising life out there while you're in here."

What the fuck? Tammy wanted to scream. Sure, she told Patrick that she wanted kids, but she didn't expect any right now. She thought she was going to have time to clear up her life first. Afterall, she took her birth control religiously to avoid this moment. Her life was already fucked up, and she was trying to mess with anyone else's – especially not her own flesh and blood.

A part of her wanted to be happy about the news he had just given her, but with her future still hanging on by a thread, she knew now was not the time. What if Detective Harris was able to put her away for good? What would happen to her baby?

"From that puzzled look on your face, I'm guessing you didn't know," he sat down in the chair directly in front of her.

"Listen, Tee, there is no reason a child should be born into this mess. I have enough to put you away forever. Patrick is going to eventually slip up, and I'll get him too. Is this really what you want for your child? You don't have a good relationship with your mom. The only person who would have loved that child like you would is dead, and with both of its parents locked up, your little one will undoubtedly end up in the system too."

The thought of her grandmother not being here for this phase in her life made her want to cry immediately.

I already feel like I haven't been able to trust Rick for a minute. Now, this bitch is telling people she had my nigga – my child's father? What if he really has shit on me and can make it stick? Will this bitch be around my fucking baby? Will Patrick even keep it? Her thoughts were starting to get louder and louder. She watched on as Detective Harris' mouth kept moving, but she couldn't focus on anything other than the thoughts pounding loudly in her mind.

"Look," Detective Harris said as he slapped a heavy manila folder on the cold, metal table. "You can continue to play this tough guy role if you want, but everyone knows you aren't ready to serve no real time. Tell me what I need to know about Patrick and the rest of your team, and I'll work out something to allow you to be there for your kid.

What's it gonna be?"

FROM THE DESK OF KEAIDY SELMON:

I really want to thank you so much for your support! Honestly, out of all of the books I've written in this series, this one has been the hardest to write. The reason Tammy's grief was able to seem so real is because this year, I lost my precious grandmother also. The hurt, confusion, anger, guilt, and shame were an honest representation of my own feelings and emotions.

For years, you all have supported the way that I can process and work through so much, and for that, I am forever grateful. I love how it seems like my struggles do not go in vain, as a lot of you all have shared similar stories with me. I think this is a great way to be reminded that we are never alone. Someone somewhere is dealing with what you are dealing with. Please never buy into the lie that no one understands or appreciates your voice. That is simply not true. The best way to heal and get to a better solution is to share our experiences and find common ground where healing can take place.

In response to some of the topics that I've addressed in this series, a lot of you have asked me to include 'Book Club Questions," and I have heard all of your requests! For this reason, you'll find some questions that you can use for your own book clubs. I was very selective about the questions that were used for a reason. Yes, this is the shortest book in the series; however, I think some compelling topics were covered in it. In this book, we addressed vengeance and the fact that while it may feel good at the moment, it can lead you to become a version of yourself that you never imagined. We talked about grief and the cycles that someone goes through after losing a loved one. We addressed envy, jealousy, hate, trauma, and how all of those things can hinder you if they are not addressed head-on. We also saw that in this game, you are not exempt from living out the consequences of your choices. I'm sure you all are tired of hearing me say this, but although we call it a game – no one wins in the end. There are people out here dying because of the poison some people are making a profit off of. It doesn't matter how much money or power you have. Control is an illusion. It's a false sense of security we give ourselves when we think 'we got it.' The reality is that the only thing you are in control of is your decisions and the person you decide to be today. You cannot control others, circumstances, or this 'game' that so many like to play around with.

I hope these discussion questions lead you to have some real, authentic, life-changing conversions. My prayer is that when you put this book down, something about you is different. If you are in need of having some of these questions answered, remember, I'm always available for your book club conversations. For more booking information, you can visit my website: Keaidy.com and send a message with your request.

Again, I want to thank you for your years of support and love. Book 4 will be out in 2022, and that is the second to last book in the series! I swear your love means more to me than I'll ever be able to put into words.

I hope ya'll know that I love ya'll like play cousins. - xo.

BOOK CLUB QUESTIONS

1. What was going through your mind when Isabella pulled out the handcuffs and roll of pink duct tape for her encounter with Kyle? Why do you think the author was intentional about mentioning those specific items?

2. In the beginning of Chapter 2, Tammy shared her feelings about losing her father to Estrella. That's when she responded with, "That's a choice that you have to be willing to make on your own. Happiness is not a place or destination; it is a choice. Once you've made that choice to get there, you have to continuously make the choice to remain happy. For now, all you have to do is cry. Cry until you don't have any tears left, and we can worry about happiness another day." Do you agree with this idea of healing through grief? Why or why not?

3. What advice would you have given Tammy at this time?

4. In Chapter 2, Tammy experiences an anxiety attack once she realized that she was going to be required to take over her father's dynasty. Have you ever experienced that yourself? If so, what kind of advice would you give to someone in that situation?

5. If you answered 'yes' to the previous question, would you be willing to talk to a therapist about that? Why or why not?

6. In Chapter 3, Tammy and Patrick finally meet up to talk. How did this make you feel?

7. Were you hoping for a reconciliation? Why or why not?

8. At the end of Chapter 3, we find out that the woman who confronted Tammy was Patrick's sister and not his lover. This shows the power of communication instead of just being so quick to cut people off based on what other people say. Do you agree with that or do you think Tammy was doing the best

she could to protect her heart by immediately cutting him off when another woman came to her 'woman to woman?'

9. At the end of Chapter 4, Kyle was given a note from his mother. How did that make you feel?

10. One of Tammy's first official orders while being in charge was trying to find Lorenzo, Estrella's long-lost lover. Did this surprise you? If it were you coming into that much power and money, what would have been your first order of business?

11. When Jason was reminiscing on Lino's final moments, he remembers a moment where Lino mentioned that no one was going to come forward with his murderer. For many years, it has been a known saying that 'snitches get stitches,' which is why Lino felt his murder would never be avenged. Do you agree with this ideology? Should we be vocal about the criminals who commit crimes, or should we speak out against the wrong that we see?

12. In Chapter 6, we find out that Tammy was in love with Kyle. Are you team Patrick or team Kyle? Why?

13. In the beginning of Chapter 7, Estrella Cruz tells Tammy, "God puts some people in your life only for a season. Some seasons may be a little longer than others, but you shouldn't cry or stress over something that you can't go back and change. You're still young and if Patrick and you don't want the same things out of life you have to do what is going to bring happiness for you now. If the two of you are meant to be together then no amount of distance or time is going to keep you two apart." Do you agree with this advice? Why or why not?

14. In Chapter 7, Tammy sees just how destructive getting revenge can be. After reading that chapter, have your views on seeking revenge changed? Why or why not?

15. After the death of her grandmother, Tammy does something

she never thought she would do: she ended two people's lives that she felt was responsible for protecting her grandmother. After the death of the first person, we immediately see that the only thing that changed was her character. She has a real moment with herself when she fell in a trance-like stance. "His body went limp faster than she would have imagined, and she wasn't prepared for the amount of blood spatter that flew out everywhere. Almost in a trance, Tammy stared in disbelief. While she had always threatened to kill anyone who crossed her, she never thought that she would be the one to do it herself.

She didn't feel the power she imagined one would feel when they ended someone else's life. Getting revenge on the man who was partially responsible for her grandmother's murder didn't make her feel any better. Instead, it scared her. Her mind raced to the fact that a little girl just lost her father to this game, just like she did. How would she ever be able to look his family in the eyes after what she just did? Knowing that she was just as cruel as Brian, she suddenly felt powerless. How had she let this game turn her into the things she despised the most? Now, she was a *murderer* on top of everything else." This moment clearly shows a distinct change in the woman that we once thought we knew. Have you ever experienced a life-changing moment that you never imagined that you would do? Does that allow you to feel sympathy for Tammy?

16. In Chapter 8, Josie says, "Tammy's personality is big on loyalty and honesty; however, her past traumas force her to create unhealthy relationships with the people that she is closest to, but her natural nature of loyalty keeps her stuck in places she doesn't need to be. Thanks to the amount of dysfunction in her past, it's the place she subconsciously finds the most peace in. That's why it's like drama can't escape her life. For example, her relationship with my brother is unhealthy. I've been telling her that for years. She won't hear me out though. Now, she really won't listen. She's experiencing PTSD from murdering those two boys, so it's almost impossible getting her to trust anyone when she is struggling to trust herself. The reason why you and Tammy seemed to be so perfect is because inside of

her is broken little girl that is still hurt from daddy issues and the broken relationship she has with her mom. Because of your past failures, you want to be a Mr. Fix It for those you care about. What most people see as strength, you recognized was nothing more than her defense mechanism. You saw that little girl who wanted love, and unlike the rejection she is used to, your loyalty to her made her feel safe. You taught her that vulnerability is a superpower and not a weakness. You allowed her to feel like she could come to you with anything without fear of consequence. It was the first dynamic, outside of her grandmother, that she's had in her life where she didn't feel the need to be a 'people pleaser' to feel secure in her position in your world. The relationship you two started opened the door for her to realize her flaws. It started the discussion of what she really wanted out of life. It was through your loyalty and honesty that she felt safe enough to admit she wanted children and marriage. Before you, she didn't think those things were possible for someone with as much trauma as she's experienced." Why do you think the author had these two characters explained in this way? Do you see yourself in either one of them?

17. Estrella was murdered before she was ever able to see Lorenzo again. Did this bring out any emotions in you?

18. Was her death something that you expected or anticipated?

19. In the beginning of Chapter 10, we find the main characters at church. The pastor says, "Now, you may be lying to yourself right now and saying that you operate out of love, but before I close this out, I want to seriously challenge how you view love. We all know 1 Corinthians 13 explains what love is. We've heard that it is patient and kind. We've heard that it isn't easily aggravated and never gives up. I've lost count of how many times I've been told that it keeps no record of wrongdoing, but how many of us can say that we can look at that entire definition of love and say that we apply that to ourselves? Because if we were honest, our thought life is rude. The way we condemn ourselves proves that we aren't willing

to suffer long or keep a clean record. Man, the way we quit the moment things get too tough shows that we aren't willing to endure every circumstance on our own. So how can we expect from others what we aren't willing to give to ourselves?" Take a moment to review that and look at how you love yourself. Do you think you are patient and kind with yourself? Do you think it's capable to show love to others that you don't show to yourself? Why or why not?

20. At the end of Chapter 10, Tammy was arrested. Were you expecting this?

21. Knowing all of Tammy's crimes and her recent revelations about herself, do you think she should be put away for good or do you think she's mentally been reformed to be a new better version of herself? If you have mercy for Tammy at this moment, do you think it would be possible for you to extend that same mercy to people currently incarcerated if you knew their story or the reason behind some of their crimes?

22. Part Three ends in the death of Isabella. We see that Patrick was so weighed down in his thoughts and emotions, that he instinctually grabbed her to shut her up. While he was lost in thought, he ended up killing the only person he knew with knowledge of what the police knew. Do you think this illustrates how dangerous being in our feelings can be? Knowing Isabella's history of being envious and jealous of Tammy, did you feel any sympathy for her death? If not, please explain why.

23. In the preview for the next book, we see that Tammy is struggling to get to a better version of herself. What changes have you seen? Do you think this is temporary because of her circumstances? Explain your answer.

24. While incarcerated, Tammy is met face-to-face with how some of her choices impacted other people. Can you think of a time in your life where you could be put in a similar situation?

25. Do you think Tammy is going to hold to the street code, or do you think she's going to 'snitch?' If you were in her position, what would you do?

ABOUT THE AUTHOR

Keaidy Selmon is a best-selling author originally from Honduras. In addition to writing, Keaidy loves inspiring other people to live out their passions. She is able to do this through her business, LexxiKhan Presents. She also has a non-profit organization that helps empower young students through art.

Keaidy loves hearing from her readers. If you are interested in booking her, or getting information on how you can help change the lives of our youth, go to her website: Keaidy.com

Also make sure to follow her on Instagram @akawords.

Made in the USA
Las Vegas, NV
29 November 2023

81803901R00059